THE VIKING GAEL SAGA

BOOK II

THOR'S WRATH

J.T.T. RYDER

Old World Heroism

First paperback edition September 2023

Book design by Nada Orlic

ISBN 978-82-94071-01-2 Paperback

Published by Old World Heroism, ENK (Norge)

www.oldworldheroism.com

Contents

"The Wise One has spoken words in the hall,
needful for men to know."

— Stanza 165 of the Hávamál, from the Poetic Edda.

CHAPTER I

The Thunder God

After the ship sailed for many vika, or sea-miles, out into the ocean, the waves churned choppier. Land faded into hazy mist that skirted the last headlands. When Asgeir looked over his shoulders, he spotted a flock of gannets heading westward, skimming the sea, while the ship followed their course. Gray sea, gray sky, gray birds. The Ocean-River widened into an endless froth. Asgeir held fast to one of the ropes of the sail, flapping like the tendrils of a squid. The sailors grasped the rigging and hoisted the sail windward. Asgeir dragged the sealskin rope close toward his body, each stroke a wince of pain from his spear wound.

Among the sailors. The wind in our sail. The open sea. His father would be proud.

"Dark clouds on the horizon," Rolf, the son of the captain, said from two men over.

"That poem from the volva, it's still with me," Vaage, another sailor said.

"Don't like it at all. We have sacrificed, but my father has a loose tongue," Rolf said.

"All for this Asgeir," Vaage said, "he's not worth the jinx. Couldn't even hold his own in the shieldwall yesterday."

"He's the son of the Gael-Slayer," Rolf said, "and he bested Arild Rudolfsson in a duel, so a wise man will speak no more."

The rope burned in Asgeir's palms as he held it with the others, his legs set against the gunwale, his face lashed by the wind.

"Go on, Vaage," Asgeir said, his hair asprawl over his face, "do you not know the sayings of the high one, Odin?"

"What is that?" Vaage asked.

Asgeir turned to him, the wind sending his hair aflutter under his hat.

"When we land, shall we redden the ring of Ullr, god of duels, Vaage?"

Vaage said nothing, but Rolf spoke.

"Calm down, Asgeir – Vaage – we are all sailors on the same ship, and Ran will drink her if we quarrel."

"Ran, you say," Vaage said and went grimfaced. The chatter quieted as the wind beat the sail like a washerwoman beating a rug.

"To Ran with your ship," Auntie Bjørg had said. She had chanted a poem that foresaw the doom of the ship's voyage when her captain, Ulf the Old, demanded that Hallgeir's sons Asgeir and Odd join his crew.

When his anger simmered, the pain in his chest rose. *That spear wound, a proud scar, but by Eir, goddess of healing, I hope she answered Saga's prayer.* He gazed upon the gray-sheened wavelets and ate his pain. At his first battle, of Borgund, a spear struck Asgeir in the chest after he had shirked away from the fight, and that led to the death of his commander, Erle. Two-way wounded, he swore to never cower from the fight again.

The warmth of the earth had faded when the Ocean-River and its spittle first soaked the men. He had earned that wound just the day before, when he shirked from the battleline and lost his mind. He paid the price of a spear piercing, and by the hand of Saga the Healer, he still lived. Asgeir clenched his teeth to stop their chattering.

"Come on, bundle up," Rolf said as they traded lines to two other sailors. They left the rowlocks to search for sea-clothes.

Soon, the men all donned their sea-clothes. Thick woolen tunics under thicker woolen jackets, needlebound mittens, leather boots, and a sealskin hood for each of them. Asgeir felt as if he had been swimming in the sealskin hood, but the gloves too were small.

They rowed on as the sea-spray battered them in the ship, and the water seeped off the hood, so it pleased him.

The sail caught the southern wind and stretched it. The ship jibed southward as the sailors rushed to the lines of the sail so that they could regain their course. The overcast sky thickened, and Asgeir wiped the rainwater from his face as they glided into the open sea. Nothing but gray ocean to all sides. Ulf had told him the sea would carve him into a man. He had only journeyed across the sea as a passenger, just a child.

The sea will make a man out of me, Ulf? I'm not afraid – Auntie said I would live, even if you all drown.

The ship rumbled as the Westwind cast a gale, and over the far horizon, a dark purple burst pulsed from the clouds. The sailor ahead of him, a young man with a scar across his bare head that creased his otherwise shiny straight hair, gawked at it fishmouthed. Some of the other rowers grumbled, and Ulf from the helm shouted as a wave crashed against the hull.

"The Sea-Bitch is a beauty," he said and tapped his foot on the deck, "built by the most skilled shipwrights in Norway. She's like any other woman. She'll treat you well if you treat her well. Calm yourselves."

Waves crested high. Sea-spray rained down on them. Frigid water splashed Asgeir in the face and ran in cold streamlets down his neck and back. Sailors unlatched their chests and flipped them open to don thicker cloaks. Asgeir peered under his stool and found no chest, just Svartganger the Lucky, his farm cat, huddled in a ball, bobbing his head.

The ship flew. No sea underneath. The sailors released their lines as the ship hit the surface again and the water pooled down around them. Sea-foam streamed in rivulets over the rails and now the ship heeled hard to the right and leaned so much that Asgeir trembled as he found himself overwhelmed by froth.

A flash. Thunder.

"Thor!" someone shouted and rolled the last sound as long as the rumble.

Thor had pounded his hammer so hard that the ship must have trembled. The rain pitter-pattered against the hull. Sheets of water fell over Asgeir's face and blurred his sight. Svartganger shot out from under the stool like an arrow in a black blotch across the awashed deck. "Hide. You may be safer somewhere else."

"We need to head back!" one of the sailors shouted from the bow.

"We press on!" Ulf shouted back from the rudder.

"This is a fucking storm!" another sailor shouted.

"Then we ride it!"

The rigging strained taut in the wind. A gale stuttered the sail, and something creaked from above. The weathervane tore off and flew away.

Before the sailors could utter a word, Ulf shouted. "Man the fucking sail!"

The sailors grabbed hold of the lines and bent into the wind. Asgeir prayed to Njordr, god of the sea, for safe passage, to protect him.

The gods will protect him, the rest of you will drown, he thought, *that's what Auntie decreed. It's what struck fear into the sailors, perhaps she smote Ulf into it, to goad him into pressing on, to refuse to turn back while lightning crackles and thunderclaps, and cast the Sea-Bitch underwater. Perhaps this is the curse of the volva.*

A hex from my lip, Bjørg said.

"The volva has cursed us," Vaage said.

"Nonsense," Ulf shouted as he walked bow-leg past him. "Helvete with that volva! We press on!"

The rain fogged the ship. Nothing but gray. Gray sea, gray rain, gray sky. Asgeir shivered, his soaked feet frozen, his hands clasped tight, ever tight around the sleek oar. They heaved, only to halt when the ship fell from the surface and landed so far down that the sail could have been under the surface of the water, but the sea pooled back and the tide took them swiftly. The sky grew darker and neither night nor day came, just rain.

"The volva's curse, we'll all drown!" Vaage said.

"Nonsense, you coward," Ulf said, and the captain gritted his teeth, shook his head, and held himself steadfast at the boom. Vaage eyed Ulf. The old sea-dog just stared back, challenging the younger but angrier man, who looked redder as he gripped the oar and rowed on.

Ulf walked to the cargo hold below the deck. He dragged up the hatch, stooped down below the deck, and emerged holding Svartganger by the scruff. The water had straggled his fur, all four legs flailed, green eyes wide.

"This is the lucky cat," he said, "and he brings us luck as he brings us mice."

"For the gods," Vaage stole up from his chest and threw something shiny into the sea. *A coin?*

"I fear not the sea," Njall, the first mate, said and pulled his sealskin hood over his head and dropped it overboard. His gray hair flattened against his head from the rain.

Soon, more sailors plucked out shiny things or undressed and cast their sea-clothes overboard. Ulf looked older and grayer in the dimlight as rainwater poured down his red nose. He stared at the cat as if appraising his value. *He'll cast him overboard!*

Asgeir elbowed through the sailors at the lines and raced across toward Ulf and snatched up a paddle. The Sea-Bitch juttered and seawater thrashed over the sailors as Asgeir shouted.

"Put him down or I'll whack you with this!"

He raised the paddle like an axeman raises his tool to chop but Ulf dropped the cat back on his feet, and Svartganger scampered away.

Ulf grabbed the paddle's shaft with both of his hands and pulled Asgeir close to him. He had hot breath, warm in the cold wind.

"Have a problem with something?"

"He's my cat, you can't throw him overboard!"

"I can throw whatever I'd like overboard," Ulf said and pulled the lad closer to him. Even drenched in seawater in the shivering ocean rain, Asgeir felt Ulf's stinky breath on his face.

"Maybe I'll throw you overboard. Maybe along with that aunt of yours."

"The Gael-Slayer would trample you under a horse," Asgeir said. The Gael-Slayer, Hallgeir, his father. A proud and known viking in his own right. "I'll not let you kill Svartganger, and I'll never forgive you for killing Odd."

"He killed himself," Ulf said. Asgeir thought to Odd in the dueling ring, when they fought the Holmgang. Asgeir and Odd against Ulf and Rolf. The bout ended with the tip of Ulf's sword in Odd's eye. He grayed to death right there.

Asgeir's grip weakened, and Ulf ripped the paddle from Asgeir's hands, nudged the butt-end of it into his chest and shoved him away an ell, then lobbed the paddle over his shoulder and into the sea.

"Man the sail."

Asgeir hastened over the slick boards and held the lines. His lips trembled and his teeth chattered as they sailed into the darkness of the storm. He caught sight of Ulf's locked chest.

After we cross the sea, Gael-Kisser will be in my sword-arm.

Lightning crackled in the distant clouds like green thread on black wool, and Ulf's horse neighed loudly at the thunderclap. The rain poured down so much that Asgeir's cold feet sat in a puddle. He had taken his hood off and cast it into the sea, along with his tunic, and wished to take his soaked pants off, too. Some of the men sailed naked, despite the coldness, for their clothes had become so waterlogged, and many had cast their sea-clothes into the sea to appease the gods.

Streamlets drained from Asgeir's nose and seeped through his lips. Gusts pummeled the sail. The winch creaked like a door hinge, and Asgeir spotted a sailor flying. A scrawny man dangled from the rope, pants around his ankles.

Asgeir pivoted and grabbed him around the chest. Asgeir's feet slid across the slippery deck and his knees banged against the gunwale. The jolt nearly caused him to let the sailor go, silent as he clung to the rope. The ship heeled to the starboardside, then portside, each gust a hammerstrike from a zestful smith.

"Help!" the sailor cried, his naked torso cold against Asgeir's. He banged both of his knees against the gunwale again when the ship bounced off the sea, but someone else tackled them back to the deck. The three men all piled in a heap of wet flesh and sealskin rope, and when they untangled it all, Asgeir saw it had been Vaage that grounded them.

"Come on, get up," Vaage said to the other sailor as Asgeir helped him up. "Good job – you saved him!"

"Thank you, two of you, real sea-wolves you are," the youngish sailor said as righted his britches and scurried off.

"Thank you, Vaage," Asgeir said as he took in a gulp of breath. "I wasn't sure if I could get a firm grip on him."

"By Njordr, we of the Sea-Bitch look after each other – back to the rigging."

The water darkened, the sky dimmed, the ceaseless rain unseen as nightfall draped over the ship as thick as felt wool. It had not been darker after Sol arced her chariot under the earth; just blackness. Sea-spray battered him as he eyed the horizonless course.

For a long while, Asgeir just held on, the lines grinding against his palms until trickles of blood seeped through his whitened knuckles. No sound but the waves and the wind. Neither pain from his hands nor chest harried him as he swung along at the command of Ulf, in a formation of sailors. There they rode the storm and Asgeir remembered little. For on that sea-horse, the trance of Njordr fell upon him, like when the Finnmen beats his drum until he shrieks in madness, or when the Ulfhednir, the wolf-warriors of yore, spear-danced with Othinn until battle-lust overcame them.

Asgeir found himself upon a gravelly beach, it all shifting underfoot as he skirted the lapping tide. He found himself colder, but strangely warm, ice and fire. Tall gray seagulls fluttered around a whirlpool just offshore, and Asgeir found himself flying toward it.

A gray wing on each of his flanks, Asgeir looked down his yellow beak over the wavelets. He glided toward the whirlpool where an elderly man stood waist-deep in the water. His voice echoed like the roar of the tide.

"Help me, Njordr," Asgeir said. "I've sacrificed much to appease you. I am so cold. I fear I am going to drown or freeze or get murdered by my captain."

"Much troubles you," Njordr said. Asgeir found himself perched upon the god's wrist like a falconer's beast. "I shall drink the Sea-Bitch, but you will be spared."

"But why?" Asgeir said. "I don't want them to drown. I like being part of the crew." He went silent. "Njordr, I need your guidance."

Njordr sang, his deep voice like a grandfather storytelling to his grandchildren.

On the vikings' field,

Thor's wrath shall yet yield.

For the volva's nephew,

Among the red sea-spew.

My gull shall guide,

Upon your watery stride.

Over the ship a doom,

But your fate a loom.
Steady your legs upon the deck,
Until the ship is wrecked.
Belt yourself with the sword,
And over enemy you will lord.

"Njordr, I don't understand. Send me a sign, so I may follow it."

"A sign you shall have."

A sunray lit the Sea-Bitch. Asgeir blinked himself awake as the sailors cheered.

"We've sacrificed enough, men!" Ulf shouted. "We'll survive this storm. We ride it like Odin rides Sleipnir. We'll cross over to Hjaltland. Perhaps we can thank this lucky cat," Ulf said, his fist tight around the rudder as he kept the ship on course over the choppy waves. "We shall carve our prow in his likeness." He took off his hat, wrung the water out, and hatted himself again.

"A dream, a vision, I don't know," Asgeir said low. "Njordr, thank you. I remember your poem. The ship will wreck, but I stay upon the deck."

Asgeir ceased shivering as the air warmed, but he became aware of his pain again, like an ache after the first seconds of awakening. He slowed as he pondered his dream of Njordr. After a spell, Svein Foul-Farter, a big, fat sailor always smitten in stench, grabbed him with his meaty hands, the man's round face weatherbeaten red.

"You're tired," he said, "and cold. We won't make it to Hjaltland before nightfall. Perhaps more. You'll be rotten before then, no good for us."

Asgeir thought rotten meant lousy at manning the sail. Under many wool blankets, sailors lay huddled together and sleeping. Asgeir crawled under and found himself pressed up against a snoring man. The ship rocked underneath him, swaying, and for a moment, he found himself naught but a babe again, his mother rocking him in his arms, swaying. The warmth of her bosom and the hearth of his home strained away from him as, did the rigging above, and the only warmth that touched him had been the tired bodies of the huddled sailors.

I wonder if I'll ever see mama again. But I know I will find papa.

Until the ship is wrecked.
Belt yourself with the sword,
And over enemy you will lord.

CHAPTER II

The Wolf Trap

Daybreak after a dreamless night came as the rain lightened. Asgeir poked his head out from the blanket to escape the odor of sweat and farts as he opened his eyes to the cloudy sky. Something furry in the crook of his elbow – *Svartganger*. The cat stretched and yawned and closed his eyes. He looked scruffier and fuzzier, and meowed in his misery.

"At least you're safe!"

"Land ho!" Njall shouted from the prow, and in an eyeblink, the ship sprung alive. The sailors hurled the blankets off themselves. Svartganger snapped up and scattered as the sailors all scrambled to their chests. Asgeir found his stool, caught up in the sudden stir. The rain had vanished now, and abeam, the scraggly flat lands of green pastures came forth.

"Hjaltland!" Ulf shouted, and the sailors cheered in a din.

"And the weather favors us! Helvete with that volva! Njordr loves us – and soon the gods will bless us with plunder in Ireland! We arrive just at the nape of winter! The Sea-Bitch rides!"

"Land, ho! Land, hey!" Ulf sung to each heave of the sailors. They scrambled to grab hold of the lines as the ship heeled into the wind.

Land, ho, land, hey!
Hardy sailors hard to slay!
Land hey, land ho!
Waves of blood as the Sea-Bitch go!

The sailors sung along until all but Asgeir sang as they rode the wind. The lands grew higher, and longer. White and dark sheep grazed on browning pastures, and chimney smoke from a longhouse at the bay-head wisped up into the overcast sky.

The song belted out as they rowed toward the bay, the shelter, where neither gale nor eddy nor storm could harry them. Safety. *At least,* Asgeir thought, *they believe that.*

Ulf apprehended Svartganger again and held him trophy-like by the scruff as he swayed in his song. "Land, ho! Land, hey! Lucky cat's gotta stay! To Northbay, hey!"

"Put him down," Asgeir said and stepped forward, but Rolf grabbed him by the arm.

"Don't spoil the mood – Svartganger is unharmed," he said.

Asgeir said nothing. Rolf's blue eyes looked forlorn as all fell silent besides the creak of the rigging and the roar of the wave.

"We haven't landed yet, Rolf."

"What say you? We've evaded Thor's smite."

"I don't believe it's over yet," Asgeir said as he lowered his voice. "Thor's wrath will be upon the Sea-Bitch. Njordr came to me in a dream."

"Your aunt," Rolf said. Njall walked behind them and put his hand on the smalls of Asgeir's back. "Go on, men, the lines! We sail shoreward!"

The sailors swayed the sail into the westwind to turn the ship southwest. The land was green and flat, with neither cap of mountain nor dent of fjord.

A wiry young man climbed up the mast and shouted something down at the sailors. The ship slowed. Ulf dropped Svartganger and he ran off.

Off in the far distance, a fire burned bright on a headland. Ulf shielded his eyes from the emerging sun. His dry skin looked deeper and gaunter as he signaled to the men. The ship slowed, and there a little boat had been rowed toward theirs. A second fire had been lit on another headland a span from that, and a third, a span from that.

"They've lit the beacons," a curly-haired, broad-nosed sailor said.

"Ulf – they think we're going a'viking," Njall said.

"We are," Ulf said, "just not here."

That meant Ireland, where the Irish petty kings squabbled like squirrels over spilled nuts. That meant plunder for vikings, who drooled over Christian gemmed, gold plated, silvered coffers.

Two wee boats sprung out from the inlet toward the Sea-Bitch, each rowed by a single man in a cowl.

"Pilots!" Rolf said with a grin. "The locals will race out with their little boats to see who reaches our ship first, and then they will navigate us through the islands. I've always wanted to see them race!"

The pilots paddled their boats apace with the other until one spindrifted, and the other kept headway toward the Sea-Bitch. The man from the winning boat laughed, and the rower sent adrift cursed in Gaelic. Asgeir understood Gaelic, for his mother hailed from Ireland. But all he could understand from the raving pilot was blackened swears.

The winner laughed again as he approached the Sea-Bitch and, ignoring the jabbering, spinning man, greeted the Sea-Bitch in Norse.

"You braved that storm! Take it you haven't been around these parts?" he said as his boat drifted toward the Sea-Bitch. Ulf, Rolf, and some other sailors had gathered up.

Ulf strummed his hand along a shield hung from the gunwale. "We're as wet as viking swords, so I have no time for prattle – are you our pilot?"

"Aye."

They tossed ropes down to the pilot's boat, he tied them to the grommets along his gunwale, and sailors raised him and his boat up onto the ship. The pilot was a grayed, older man with a leathery face.

"I'm Hamish and I speak Norse," he said with a thick twang.

"Doesn't matter if you speak our tongue – we have a Gaelic speaker," Ulf said and nodded over to Asgeir. "How far will you pilot us?"

"Where are you voyaging?"

"Ireland."

"I've piloted Kjetil Flatnose once to the South Isles – the current at Cape Wrath nearly tore his drakkar apart. We can't round the Cape this late in the year."

"Then go and fetch the loser of your race, he is probably eager to help."

"What do you offer then?"

"An Irish slave-girl," he said and gestured toward Éabhín. She had been huddled against the mast, near Ulf's horse. Her mouth dropped and she stuttered in protest.

Éabhín! He can't just trade her off!

The girl had been won by Ulf from her master, Kjetil Redcloak, after he defeated his men in a raid. Kjetil had insulted Ulf, while his wife and friend plotted to murder him. Thus Ulf showed Kjetil the length of his spear, and took his horse, slave, and head. Asgeir wished to buy her to free her, but Ulf appraised her worth too high.

"She has wide hips, good to bear me a grandson," Hamish said. "We drop her off now, and I can pilot you the full route to Ireland. I even have some friends in Dubh Linn."

"We have a deal."

Asgeir met the eyes of Ulf, his gray eyes twinkled in the sunlight when they fell upon Asgeir.

"What, you want to hump the Gael girl?" Ulf shouted. "I bought her, therefore I own her, go stick your cock up your own ass if it behooves you – and let's not even mention that aunt of yours, battering my men in superstition! And look what you made me do, shouting in front of our pilot!"

Ulf spoke again to Hamish. "She's yours, pilot."

Éabhín sat blank faced. Asgeir just sat there. He turned his head toward the chest of Ulf, where his sword, Gael-Kisser, lay. *Someday, I'll be the captain, Ulf.* Head held high, he paced back over to his stool and sat and stuck the oar hard into the waves.

"Just what do you care anyway?" Éabhín said in Gaelic to Asgeir as he walked back to his seat.

"You deserve better," he said, "you're not a slave."

"Aye, and someday, they'll pray to their heathen gods in sorrow that they mistreated me so."

"Landward," Ulf said.

The ship approached the still-watered bay. The sailors manned the oars. Asgeir's shaking, unsteady legs bounced against the stern legs of his stool.

The starboard rowers steered the ship eastward and then past a series of small houses that dotted the shoreline. Hamish whistled and waved his arms, and another man came rowing out to him. The oarsmen stroked their blades into the calm sea as they neared land.

Hamish waved Éabhín over, a grin on his gray-bearded face. He put an arm around her and said in Gaelic, "My son is handsome and strong, and you'll be safer than among these vikings."

Éabhín was lowered down into the boat with another Gaelic man, an older one, speaking to Hamish in his tongue. The old man nearly jumped when he laid eyes on Éabhín. "These heathens don't deserve such an Irish beauty," he said. Hamish agreed, and the old man rowed Éabhín away from the Sea-Bitch and shoreward.

Éabhín turned to the ship and shouted, "Farewell, you vikings! Best of luck finding someone as good as I am at sewing – and the lot of ya are much less prettier without me!"

Asgeir sighed as her red hair bobbed along the choppy bay. *No parting words from her to me. I guess she disliked me as much as the rest of the crew. Slave or not, Thor, protect you, or that Bride goddess you call upon, good Éabhín.*

The Sea-Bitch left the inlet, and Hamish guided Ulf to steer southward. They bypassed dryrocks, the waves crashing over them as wild as a spooked horse, and Asgeir thought of the ship's hull grinding against it until the boards split. With a silent prayer to Njordr from him, the ship sailed out of the bay. Asgeir overheard the captain and pilot speaking when they spoke downwind.

"Tell you what, Ulf," Hamish said as he chewed on some tar. "That Irish girl was too pretty for this. I'll do you a favor. The youngest daughter of Jarl Toke seeks a suitor. Your son could guest in his house at Ronaldsay, the southernmost isle – I have friends there to welcome him."

"Very well then, Hamish, I suppose you Gaels are a warm people," Ulf said, also chewing gum. "My lad will surely seduce the Jarl's daughter. That quarrelsome Harald will have yet another bulwark against him if he tries to unleash his hounds in the Northern Isles."

Ulf spoke of Harald Finehair, a king who had declared no pair of snips shall touch his hair until all Nordmenn unite under one king – him.

"You hear that, son? We're leaving you off when we reach Orkney."

"When we reach Orkney? Ulf, you're in Orkney."

Ulf laughed. "You hear that, men, that storm blew us off course! We're in the Orkneys! The Jarl's very seat! To Helvete with that volva! To Helvete with her curse! We rode the storm south, and now we're even closer to Ireland! Njordr loves us!"

The sailors cheered around Asgeir. They belted into a song as they rowed, though Rolf turned to him and they spoke.

"Looks like I've lucked out," he lowered his voice, "if she'll sink."

"I'm glad for you, my friend," Asgeir said. "My dreams have strengthened like oiled iron. I'm afraid my aunt is right." He sighed as he scanned the crew of rowers, and his eyes rested upon Ulf. "Even if I don't want her to be right."

"We've ridden the storm," Rolf said with a sucked-in sob. "We've stayed on course in spite of the stormy winds, the lightning, the overflowing waves. Why would the gods punish us now?"

"So long as Ulf is captain," Asgeir said.

"Let's talk about this no more. I cannot fathom my father drowning, and all of our friends certainly deserve a more fitting end. I suppose the Norns have spun me a different yarn." He sighed and gazed toward the featureless green coast.

"I just hope she's pretty, and kind, and loves me."

The Sea-Bitch hugged the coast until they rowed into another bay where a hall sat at a beachhead. As the ship neared the beach, Ulf and Rolf spoke much amidships. When the Sea-Bitch landed and skidded up the gravel, the sailors all began to embrace the captain's son, one by one.

Asgeir stood to meet Rolf. He had his shield strapped across his back, and he had armed himself with his spear in one hand, and he led the reins of Ulf's horse with the other. When he spotted Asgeir, his eyes went big and he dropped his spear and the reins, and embraced Asgeir.

"By Njordr – we've come to an end here," Rolf said as he ruffled Asgeir's hair.

Asgeir had embraced him back, but held his hands aloft, when he remembered Rolf's strikes and stabs and pivots against him and Odd, back on that gray islet.

"I sure hope she has a fieryness to her," Asgeir said with a quivered lip, "and you'll like her."

"Good journey to you," Rolf said and let him go, picked up his spear, took the reins of the horse, and walked down the ramp off the Sea-Bitch.

"This is no farewell. My son will sail with us again. We move on."

I think I'll miss him. But Ulf is right – we'll meet again, Rolf.

Some of the men there at the beachhead, shirtless with dark hair, shoved the prow of the Sea-Bitch, and it slid back into the sea. The sailors portside rowed, Asgeir along with them. He heard the workmen there, thralls, speaking in a tongue he could understand vaguely. Picts, the islanders before the Norse had arrived.

After many vika, the sky lightened, high afternoon came, and the wind settled so that they had to row. They rowed past many isles, a broken chain of them like a shattered pot, and when they reached a headland at the end of the island, a little boat with four rowers met them there.

Ulf and Hamish met them from over the rail starboardside.

After a short spat between the two parties, dampened by the howls of the wind so Asgeir couldn't hear, Ulf came back in a huff, stomping his feet, and signaled to the sailors to turn.

"A landing tax – and to think, we are kin with the Norsemen of the Orkneys," Ulf said. "To Helvete with that. We're not paying."

"We can cross the isthmus, Ulf," Hamish said. "It'll take some effort to lug her overland, but the isthmus will keep us away from the worst of the currents and the wind."

"Onward, men, we cross the isthmus!"

With some grumbles, the portside ceased rowing, the ship steered, and in a long arc, changed course. The sail caught the westward wind now and gained speed. Seagulls flew overhead as the ship hugged the coast.

Foul-Farter dropped a slither of salted pork in the lap of Asgeir. He chewed it and delighted in its saltiness. From the coast, a trio of men in undyed tunics with a flock of sheep looked on at them.

"Your first time across the sea in a storm?" he asked Asgeir.

"That was scary," Asgeir said, but regretted it.

"A smooth sea won't make a good sailor!"

"I sailed before, a lot, with my father."

"Just fjords. Fjords are easy. I can sail a fjord as easy as I can belch. Not where we are going. It's dangerous. The span between high and low tide is as long as a goat jumps. Lots of dryrocks and reefs. And the winds. They are like women. Can't foreknow what they will do."

Asgeir sniffed a bit. He remembered waking up many times in the night due to the stench of the man.

"You know, you stink. You woke me up with your farts."

Svein laughed. "Why else that nickname? Kept you warm, didn't I?"

"I wasn't cold."

Foul-Farter raised his bushy eyebrows. "That means you were freezing to death," he said and left as a sailor beckoned him over. Something hung over Asgeir, like stiff air before a heavy rain.

I could have died, but I still live. What has fate spun for me?

Asgeir chewed on his pork as he rowed. The day passed. They went by many harbors with long farmhouses, just as they had been built back in Hordaland. Each house lay near an older house, often roofless, but always of hewed stone and rounded. There were many ruins of tower-like buildings along the coast, strange and giant, some as tall as twenty men.

The lands on both sides of the ship hemmed in, the sea narrower. A narrow, grassy shred of land divided the North Sea from the Atlantic. They had come to the portage.

The ground of the isthmus had been carved, boat-shaped, to allow the sea-vessels to be dragged up onto them. The *Sea-Bitch* slowed as its bow reached the dragging-place. A handful of men, all in undyed tunics, scurried forth from the nearby hills.

"Disembark – where are the porters? Is that it?" Ulf said as he pointed at the men onshore.

One of the men, with a long black mustache, waved his bronzed arms at the sailors as they dropped a rope ladder over the ship's portside.

"Jarl Toke isn't home," the man onshore said in broken Norse.

"Where is he?"

"Somewhere around Pictland," he said. "He'll be back soon, but no seacraft can go over unless he agrees."

"To Helvete with that," Ulf said. "We'll pay you proper for passage."

"We still can't do it."

Ulf unsheathed his sword in a rasp, and the mustached man winced.

"We'll do it," the Pictish man said.

"Yes, you will."

The sailors climbed out of the ship along with Asgeir. The shore had been rocky, with mossy black walls that lined the slipway. An otter glided into the sea as a blur as Asgeir found himself on green land again. He might have dropped down to kiss it.

The men of the isthmus split into two groups. Nearby, some simple wooden storage houses, and next to it, a bunch of long logs under a taut awning. The mustached men uncovered it, and Ulf gestured toward the logs, as two of the men came down from the hills leading two large brown horses.

"Are they speaking Gaelic?" Svein asked Asgeir as he grabbed a log and nodded to the lad to help.

"No, they're Picts."

"You don't understand the Pictish tongue?"

"Not really. It's too different from Gaelic."

The sailors aligned the logs in a row of shaven trunks across the isthmus, while the Picts tied the horses to the ship. With Ulf on a hillock and nodding along, the horses dragged the Sea-Bitch over the first log, and it rolled onto the second, and when it had come to the last log, the sailors plucked it from the sandy ground and dropped it in the front. The horses pulled hard as they crested the isthmus, and when they reached the other side, another slipway had been dug half-man deep into the ground.

Ulf stood with a crate and gestured the two eldest Picts over. The Picts opened it. The mustached man shook his head.

"We need wood, not wheat," he said.

"What man would turn away wheat?"

"We have wheat, we need wood."

"Timber? Lumber? Beams? A door? What do you need?"

"Anything, there aren't many trees on Orkney."

"We need our wood for repairs and fires and suchlike."

"Wood or nothing."

"The thrall bargains?" Ulf said with a gap-mouthed grin. "You get nothing, then."

The Pict wrung his mouth.

"My master will be angry."

"Your master can kiss my ass."

Ulf hectored his men back onto the ship as Asgeir pushed with nine other sailors the *Sea-Bitch* back into the calm bay on the other side of the isthmus. They all clambered into the ship and rowed out. As they did, Ulf snarled. Asgeir turned his head and found a dirty Pictish rear-end facing the ship.

"Fetch me my bow and quiver," Ulf said to Njall, who failed to respond. Ulf turned to another sailor.

"Fetch me my bow and quiver now!"

The sailor returned with a bow and a leather quiver with a handful of goosefeathered arrows. Ulf nocked an arrow and pulled the bowstring tight to his ear, left eye closed. He loosened the arrow in a twang. The mooning Pict turned to find the arrow checking off the greened stone wall that lined the slipway. He bent over again. Ulf nocked an arrow, loosened it, and the bowstring twanged. The arrow plunged into the sea a foot before the slipway. A third arrow now, high-arced as the ship and that landed in the gloom of the green grass. The Pict shook his rear end and slapped his ass-cheeks ruddy.

"Just leave it, captain," Njall said to Ulf.

"This is a grave insult. In front of my sailors."

"He's just a thrall."

"That makes it worse."

The ship coursed northwestward along the coast as the isthmus faded, but Ulf refused to halt his stare, his frown deepened until his leathery skin crevassed. His mouth gapped open and he shouted at the portside crew.

"Halt! Steer, and turn!"

The ship reversed course, some of the sailors grumbling. Asgeir knew their muscles strained, their bellies throbbed, their clothes were still half-soaked.

"We should really let it go," Njall said.

"Who's the captain here?"

The *Sea-Bitch* rowed back toward the isthmus. The Picts had left, but one young man lifted his head out from some scrub on a hill to the east. He started down the slope. Ulf unslung his bow from his arm, loaded an arrow, and shot at the Pict. The thrall crumbled to his knees, goosefeathers ruffling in the breeze from the arrow that stuck out of his chest.

"Moon me, will you?" he yelled downwind, and his voice echoed about the cluster of storage buildings at the isthmus. With a gesture to the portside, the *Sea-Bitch* reversed course again. Just as Asgeir heaved the last stride, a horn blew from back at the isthmus.

The Pictish thralls rolled the logs down the slope of the isthmus toward the slipway as a light-red striped sail emerged over the isthmus. At least twenty-seven men pushed a ship, longer but thinner than the *Sea-Bitch*. They had not bothered to rope the draft horses. Three bowmen came first, eying the *Sea-Bitch*, and gauged the range.

"Looks like their master is angry," Njall said.

"We can parley," Ulf said, "if they want a fair toll."

"No Ulf," Njall said, and the short man stood on his heels. "I tire of this! They're not coming to parley! That's a larger and faster ship than ours, and they have more oarsmen – and we're all tired!"

"Helvete," Ulf said, "then we leave. Row! We'll out-row them."

The captain threw his long gray hair over his shoulder, then his fringed red cloak over as well, and pointed toward the dusky horizon.

"Row, fast, what, are you little girls?"

The men rowed hard, Asgeir stiffened his legs and threw his hips into it, as Rolf had shown him. His spear wound pulsed, but he feared worse wounds if the master of the Picts caught them. The *Sea-Bitch* glided, but the warship slid down into the bay at the isthmus. The rowers there, thirty-five at least, rowed, and their ship glided. They unfurled an ocean-colored green-blue striped sail. They caught the southerly wind and jetted forward like a cat bursting in a hunt. It was a karve, Asgeir knew, a warship, for his father owned one down on Eigg.

The carved prow of the karve came into view. A spewing sea-serpent. Asgeir looked over his shoulder to find the ship had gained on them. The *Sea-Bitch* coursed but the karve glided, and in haste, the sailors of the Sea-Bitch strained as the sea opened around them.

"We won't make it," Njall said to Ulf.

"They couldn't hit the broadside of a whale from..."

An arrow hissed into Njall's back, and he fell face-down to the deck in a sigh. Asgeir gasped as he watched first mate Njall Gray-Hair lying in an oozing pool of blood.

"Njall!"

Vaage put a hand on his shoulder. "He's dead, man."

Holm returned to Asgeir, where Odd had lain on his back. Now Njall lay on his belly. *Ulf, his blood is on you, you're so reckless... Njall, farewell, my friend, my teacher, my brother-in-arms.*

Ulf gaped at Njall's lich for a spell. "They killed you, my old friend."

He swayed like he ripped himself out of a trance and yelled "Truce!" as his feet tracked Njall's blood about the deck.

"Truce!"

An enemy sailor yelled something back in a different tongue.

"You speak Gaelic!" Ulf said to Asgeir.

"Yes."

"Tell them we'll parley!"

"I don't speak that language."

"It's Gaelic!"

"It's not."

"Helvete!" Ulf said as he ducked under the rigging. Another arrow clanked off the rudder. "Men, the din of the Valkyries is upon us – fight!"

The wind buffeted the sail of the Sea-Bitch as it slowed, and Ulf shouted commands upwind. A trio of Sea-Bitch sailors nocked arrows and fired at the ship. All three of their targets plunged into the gray, choppy ocean. A hail of arrows returned from the karve.

Asgeir dove under the little three-legged stool. A sharp, iron arrow pierced through the seat and struck him in the arm. Blood oozed down. He looked over himself to find more stings, but remained otherwise unscathed. He crawled on his belly away from the bow, the stool as a shield over his head.

Sailors raced to and fro about the deck, leather-shod feet like discordant drumming all about the deck. The starboardside of sailors steered the ship broadside toward the karve, while the portside had dropped their oars and formed a line of spears and shields. Asgeir, onlooking from behind a yawning chest, found the foemen all had green-blue striped shields just as their sail. Their karve bestrode the *Sea-Bitch*, javelins poised at them.

Something stunk, even above the sea-salt and sweat and amidst the rattling of iron. Foul-Farter. He pulled Asgeir up and shoved a javelin in his hands.

"Where's your shield?" Svein asked.

"I don't have a shield."

"Pull it off someone dead. You ever throw a javelin?"

"Only for fun."

"You'll have fun now," he said with a half-grin, his fat cheeks squinting his small dark eyes.

Ulf had vanished for a while, but returned now, clad in his shimmering chainmail. He unsheathed Gael-Kisser, his shield aloft, and pushed through his men to get to the center of the line.

"Javelin range!"

Ulf's men aimed their javelins above their shoulders.

"Cast!"

The javelins arced through the sky like seagulls after spilled food on the beach. At the same moment, the enemy's volley arced in return.

Asgeir had thrown his javelin, but he did not know where it landed. A big round shield wheeled upward in front of him. A javelin clanked to the deck in front of his feet, checked right off the iron boss. He could smell who did it.

"Thank you, Svein! My father will repay you!"

"Get a shield!"

Asgeir found a youngish sailor in a rust-colored hood askew over his face lying on his back. A javelin had struck him through the neck. He grabbed the warm hand of the dead man, and one by one, pried the quivering fingers off the handle. He hid behind his shield as more javelins shot through the sky; one flew over his head, struck a sailor, who tripped over something and spilled out over the deck and into the sea below.

Before Asgeir could react, a grinding sounded underfoot. Harsh, rumbling, squeaking as a giant's quernstone. The two ships had collided, and now the starboardside of the Sea-Bitch and the portside of the karve rasped against each other.

"Forward!" Ulf shouted. "The valkyries fly tonight!"

One rank of men each the ships had, and these ranks approached each other spear-first. Asgeir found himself near Vaage. He pulled his hand out from under his spear and grabbed the shaft overhand. Asgeir, who had found a cast javelin, followed his lead. The javelins now worked as spears, onehanded, with shields, and both sides jabbed and struck at each other. Iron met wood, the drumming of spearpoints against leather-covered shields and their iron bosses.

Vaage held his spear aloft, his shield forward, and when the foemen in front of him turned to stab someone else, he stabbed him in the shoulder and pulled his own spear back. The enemy winced and slumped out of the line.

"Wait for when they are not looking," Vaage said to Asgeir, but then dove back a foot and back into the line and stabbed, but his foeman blocked with his shield. "But fucking watch out!"

Asgeir waited. His enemies stood taller than him. Most a head taller. He knuckled the shaft so hard an ache strained up his forearm. Every time he raised his elbow to strike with the spear, a spear came for him. He jumped back out of its way, then back into the line.

"Axe!" someone shouted. Asgeir turned to look but then something grabbed the rim of his shield in a thud. A man in a bloody hemp tunic with an iron-headed axe had caught the rawhide border of Asgeir's shield. The axeman heaved, the axe's beard dug through the leather of the shield and splintered the wood, the rawhide strained on its waxed linen threads. Asgeir let go and flung backward as the axeman ripped the shield away. Vaage had wheeled his shield in front of him and blocked a spearman's strike.

The axeman swung his weapon around and in a thud, grabbed Foul-Farter's shield. Foul-Farter farted loud as he pulled himself back, nearly a step back from Asgeir. The axeman's upper arm bulged as spittle flew over his gray beard. Asgeir lobbed his javelin at him.

The tanged iron-tip checked off the axeman's shield, but the axeman had looked down at the spear. Vaage then lunged forward, the beard of the axe still hugging his shield-rim, spearpoint aimed at the axeman. The spear grazed across the neck of the foe. He released his axe, and Vaage stumbled back, caught his balance, and skewered his spear right into the belly of the axeman. He gurgled, and his comrades shoved him back out of the line.

A tall, lean foe left the enemy line, unslung a horn from his neck, and blew into it. The horn mooed like a cow. *I've done it,* Asgeir thought, *I distracted him and Vaage got him. I think.*

More grinding, but from the prow. The Sea-Bitch shuddered and even rose. The hull screeched, and then something rammed amidships that tossed the sailors around the deck. Asgeir tripped backward and ended up slamming against a chest back-first. The sailors of the karve let out a peal of laughter as their craft pried away from the *Sea-Bitch.*

They had all drifted toward a small harbor, where the foam splashed over hard black things in the water. Dryrocks, jagged above the surface, the maker of countless shipwrecks.

The *Sea-Bitch* tore across the black rocks, the body of the ship keening like mourning Gaelic women as the dryrocks ripped open the hull. The sailors scrambled around the deck. Most had dropped their weapons. One man dove overboard, and another, and another. Two of them came back up in the brine. Asgeir looked to and fro and found some sailors on their knees, others diving overboard, some swimming landward, while yet others swam toward the enemy karve.

Asgeir found Ulf at the rudder with a hand on it, a wet-bladed spear in his other hand, eyes averted back toward Norway.

"That rotten wench of a volva," he said as he found Asgeir, who attempted to steady himself on the rocking, soon-to-be-reeling ship. "A pox on her."

"I should take you down with my ship," he said to Asgeir, one slow step at a time. The ship slammed against the dryrocks again, now starboard, and threw Asgeir down. The deck was caked in blood over cracks in the planks. Rivets strained and crackled. The ship felt too still.

The darkening sun cast a shadow over Asgeir in the shape of a man with a long, raised tentacle. The sword of Ulf the Old. The old sea-captain had nothing behind his eyes, just a blankness, as frigid brine lapped over Asgeir. Something hissed nearby. The rigging?

"The volva's curse," Ulf said, "my ship sinks and we drown, but you survive. To Helvete with that. To Helvete with that!"

Ulf twisted his wrist in a stab down at the quivering chest of Asgeir. The sword-point cleft his flapping long blond hair. The flat of the blade slid down his head as Ulf screamed, holding something on his face.

Svartganger!

The soaked cat had been all claws and teeth as it wailed like a wayward cartwheel, its tail fluffed out as it harried the sea-captain. Ulf spun and turned and slipped on some bloody water, but righted himself, and raised his hand to smite the cat.

Asgeir tackled Ulf's left leg, his knee bent awkwardly, and the old man, the Viking-Gael, the sword, and the cat all piled into a heap on the cracking deck. The sky whirled like yarn on a reel.

Svartganger leapt off the face of ruddy Ulf. The captain climbed to his feet, his sea-journeyed legs steady as the cat scampered to the side of Asgeir, who rolled up and pivoted from Ulf.

If I am to die, I want my father's sword around my waist.

Asgeir seized Gael-Slayer off the slick boards of the deck as Ulf approached him.

Ulf, mouth gaped open and eyes fixed on nothing, halted. The deck cracked out from underneath him and he plummeted to the depths below. Asgeir found no time for thoughts as the old sea-captain vanished.

Asgeir snatched up Svartganger, who clung to his face by his claws, the green eyes of the cat wide as it shivered against his sweaty, wet, bloody chin and nose.

The lid of Ulf's chest flapped as the Sea-Bitch trembled. He shoved a hand through the gap and flipped it open. A chest barreled past them and splashed into the sea. *The Sea-Bitch* quaked now; half of it had already sunk.

He unlatched the chest as the sea slurped and sucked against the hull. He pulled out the red-leathered scabbard and belted it around him thrice because his father had girth, and tied it tight and sheathed the sword. All the while barrels and bags and crates and men slid off the deck and into the choppy sea. The enemy ship had rowed away and now just waited adrift, a din of jeers from the enemy ship.

Sword-belted, Svartganger clinging to his face, Asgeir sat against the chest. gray sea, gray sky, gray-faced dead sailor at his feet. The man had slit his own throat rather than drown, and his blood drained into the rising sea around them. To his left, the open ocean, to his right, an inlet. *I'll drown with the rest of the crew.* Nothing remained on the adornless, peopleless, motionless ship besides Asgeir and Svartganger, the cat clinging to his leg. He petted the cat, peeled him from his trousers, and cradled him like a baby. "We will live together, my friend."

He leaned his head skyward. Everything grayed.

"Njordr, I stay on the ship as you commanded."

The sailors from the enemy karve belted out a rolling song. Asgeir could not understand it. Was it Pictish?

His teeth chattered as he found himself floating at the surface of the ocean. The ship bent under the weight of the surge as the tide took him. Svartganger dug his claws into his face as he swam shoreward. Something seemed to grab his feet and pull him down. The sword in its sheath? No, a sailor had grabbed his leg, but his grip was too frail, and he sank into the murk.

Asgeir stroked away from the sinking ship as a wave crashed over his face. Something slithered under him, and he grabbed it. *The stool!* He clung to it much like Svartganger clung to him, and they floated. Each rope of the Sea-Bitch's rigging snapped one by one, and the mast cracked and broke in half and the sailcloth submerged into the sea as if being washed. The realm of Ran drank the last chunk of the *Sea-Bitch* in one drought.

Under the dusky sky, Asgeir found himself drifting shoreward. He kicked his legs the best he could, all soundless. Svartganger, the drowned men, even the wind lulled into a breeze.

Ran had taken her toll on the *Sea-Bitch*, and made a graveyard of that quiet bay.

Asgeir kicked until something scraped him underfoot. A rock. He kicked past it and found another, and jammed his toes but he had no time for pain. He found a rocky seabed, and hopped from rock to rock as if he pranced through the water.

Sea above his neck, then his chest, stomach, waist, knees; he washed ashore on a sandy gravel beach. He sat there at the ebb, the ocean calm, the karve rowed to avoid the dryrocks that had battered the Sea-Bitch. The stool washed up alongside him. He dragged it across the beach, set it upright, and sat down. He petted the soaked pelt of Svartganger until the cat eased off his bleeding face, slid down, and stood on his lap shivering. The cat poured out one long, sorrowful meow.

"Auntie, did you really curse that ship?"

To Ran with your ship,
A hex from my lip,
To me the waves heed,
In the gray great mead

Asgeir recited Bjørg's poem as the ship shadowed the sun when it reached shallow waters. Coughing, his heart racing, all four of his limbs as heavy as boughs, he found himself unable to slide off the stool. *They're going to kill me, and I cannot even die on my feet.*

The ship shadowed the setting sun. Much chatter arose from the enemy's deck as they hoisted the sail. The keel ground against the rocky shorebed, Svartganger shirked away, but settled back upon Asgeir's lap and quaked. Sunrays peaked beyond the now thin mast to reveal them.

A gaggle of Ulf's sailors stood roped on the ship. Bedraggled, drenched, shivering in a mass and held at spearpoint by a duo of shirtless Picts. Some other men lay lifeless, leaned against the keelson. The shadows moved about, and a few climbed down from the karve.

I must flee. But my legs won't move. They're too heavy. He struggled to move his feet, tar-like. With a lurch, he leaned backward and found a darkened flat farmstead a hundred or so paces off, a boathouse nearby, and a herd of sheep half-grazing, half-looking.

Asgeir was just an onlooker as they waded through the water toward him. Nine men, their sea-wet hair jagged like the spiky hair of trolls.

Shivering, teeth chattering, quaking, he looked as the men reached him. A gruff, filthy Pict brandished rusty iron fetters.

"Just let me take him," Asgeir said between a gulp of air. "The cat."

The men said nothing when the iron collar clamped around his neck, cold but somewhat loose. The same Pict tugged on the chain, but Asgeir landed on his chest. The cat pivoted to dart away, but a sailor snatched him up by the scruff. That sailor had ashy blond hair under an askew hat with a brim, and a mustache that didn't quite connect to his beard.

A white-bearded, robust man kneeled over at Asgeir. His shoes looked too waxy to have just trudged through seawater. He reached down toward the brass buckle of Gael-Kisser's scabbard.

"No, that's my father's sword."

"That's the sword for the gods," he said, his thick black mustache curled over his lips. His face flushed, his eyes tired, his movements slow. "You risked it for spoils, now it becomes the spoils."

He unbuckled the scabbard from Asgeir, who shoved his hand down, but his weakness left him meek, and the pithy man just shoved his hands away. The wet leather belt fell off his waist and a sailor took it from the beach.

The burly man scooped Asgeir up and hauled him back toward the karve.

"And you too, the spoil."

Asgeir gasped and now all thoughts rushed to him. "It was Ulf the Old's blunder, not mine."

"You can't escape the law, viking," the burly man said, his voice as husky as his frame. "Tyr's justice shall come to you. Woe to the defeated. Woe to those who cannot escape."

Upon the karve, the bearded man dumped Asgeir off his shoulders. Asgeir landed on deck and winced, and found himself with a pool of blood rolling over him in a rhythm with the tides. The brim-hatted man dropped Svartganger into a green wool bag and closed its wooden handles shut.

Nine of Ulf's sailors survived as prisoners. Most with downcast gazes, glassy eyes, and expressionless faces, they had been tied together with a zigzag of rope. Among them, Asgeir could smell Foul-Farter, and spotted the flat-faced sailor, but he knew the rest not so well.

The sailors piled three dead men into a heap, bloody water rolling about the deck like after a flood. Some thralls bucketed it out as the sailors sat upon their chests and rowed away from the inlet.

"I'm the son of the Gael-Slayer," Asgeir said to the bearded man. "Grant me mercy."

"You receive no mercy when you are merciless."After a spell, he spoke as the sail unfurled and the sailors pulled the ropes taut to catch the Westwind.

"I'll have none of this viking business. The jarl himself tasked me to ensure no raiding happens. Not when Harald is sick of this turmoil so much that he threatens our freedom. The jarl will not have it. Harald will not have it. I will not have it."

"My father is Hallgeir, huskarl to the King of Lothlend," Asgeir said. "He will pay handsomely for me."

"I told you that it does not matter. You're the spoils. You've been unlucky, for some of your fellow vikings escaped, though the unluckier ones lie dead on my karve or they've taken a watery grave. Whatever the Norns have spun for you is my victory. Now, men, we sail for Jarl Toke's farm, with new farmhands."

My father will get me out of this – we're not far from his home now. Ulf, blast you, blast your temper, to Helvete with your soul!

You did go down with your ship, like a man.

Asgeir turned toward the inlet there.

The sky yellowed as twilight sprinkled the sea in blue, while the sun threatened to wink beyond the horizon.

There, upon the shadowed shore of the inlet, something crawled out of the sea. It had straggles like strips of clothes wagging behind it. It moved with all the grace of the afterwalker, the dead that rose again to walk to haunt the living. Just as Asgeir fixed his eyes upon its scraggled form, the ship turned southward.

Ulf, you've bestowed a worse curse upon me than my aunt has your ship.

And memories – to my friends of the Sea-Bitch!

CHAPTER III

The Third Son of Rig

Over the darkened sound, the ship rowed into an inlet, nameless and featureless. Black sea. Black sky. Black blood dried across the deck of the ship. The smells of the burdened beasts, the sweat of the men, and the gore of the wounded and dead on board all clung to the wind. Asgeir's teeth clattered as he shivered from the ice-cold water he had just managed to escape. *Ran's realm.*

They stood tied up in a cluster around the mast, their forms as dull as the cloudy night.

Thoughtlessness harried him. Dreamless sleep came and went in spells for Asgeir, the heaviness of the battle and swim and capture weighed upon him and forced him asleep. When the karve left shore at first light, he woke while chained to the mast, the unknown a haze about him on all sides. All the while he gripped his rusty collar until it dug into his palms. He gazed upon the mass of men, the captured crew, but couldn't make out their features in the darkness.

The crew. The crew is here. Some men overcame the waves. Ulf drowned, the old sea-wolf drunk by the daughters of Aegir. But there're living men here.

"Men, we overcame the drowning of the Sea-Bitch. We're alive. Come on! Where's her crew's song?"

None responded. One choked as he squirmed among the clump of bloodied and bruised flesh.

"Come on," he said to them, and craned his neck to cast a glance at them. Dawn rosed the sky over the desolate deck. The captives stood silent. Asgeir caught the whiff of a familiar scent from one man huddled with them.

"Svein."

Svein said nothing. He closed his eyes and lolled his head back. Asgeir knew him because he stood a head taller than his comrades, with his tangle of black hair bobbed at the nape of his neck.

"I could still smell you," he said with a chuckle. "Cheer up, we've been through worse dangers. Don't you remember, Svein? Don't you remember when Arild caught us in his trap? Don't you remember how Thor defended us that day? What of when Tyr granted us justice? Or when Odin... demanded?"

How could I ever return my honor, to be brave in battle, when I am a captive? No, I will not be a captive for long. I am the son of the huskarl of the King of Lothlend, and all will know my land-right.

"Come on, how did the song go? Ho! blood flows where the Sea-Bitch goes!"

"End it," a dark-haired sailor said with a sigh. "Just let me rest."

He cast a glance over to the bag in which Svartganger lay in a lump. *At least you're still the same, my friend.*

The morning passed. Asgeir found himself in a stupor that neither dream nor thought crossed. The humidity rose until he found himself even wetter than from the drizzle above from sweat.

A pair of Picts down at the wooden dock below the ship spoke, and Asgeir awoke to their surly voices and listened the best he could.

"The winter hag slacks off," one said, but Asgeir could hardly understand the second's sentence. *I must know my fate.*

"Could you say that again?" Asgeir called out in Gaelic. "I can almost understand what you say –slower?"

Neither of the Picts responded.

"Answer me," Asgeir said in Gaelic, slow, but then in Norse: "I'll speak the tongue of your masters, if you prefer."

A Pict thudded over the rail. He had a pointed beard, like a goat's, much meat around the eyes covered with stringy black hair.

"What did you say?" he said in garbled Norse.

"We can nearly speak to each other," Asgeir said. "I speak slow – you understand."

The Pict punched Asgeir in the ribs. With a wheeze, Asgeir curled up and slapped his feet on the deck as the Pict disembarked the ship.

"Coward, punches a man chained," he said between breaths.

"What would Ulf say?" he asked the sailors.

None said a word. It rained, and the mist covered the shores of the quiet bay. After a spell, a white-bearded man boarded the ship with the Pict that had pummeled him. A red-bearded, black-haired man poked his head over the rail behind them.

"That one, Audun," said the same Pict, in Norse, "the one with the dog collar. He's a Gael, I reckon."

"That Gaelic-speaking troublemaker? Is that him, Earp? A viking Gael? He'll work for you, Eirik."

"Why me?" the man with the short-cropped red beard asked. He had a wide face, and a glee in his blue eyes like a cheerful troll. His straight black hair danced just above his shoulders.

"Because he won't get away with squeaking in his own tongue, not without you or your loyal thralls. Don't you want that?"

"I agree," Eirik said, "I feel my farm barren, especially with Jarl Toke missing. I would rather have fighters at my side."

"You'll have fighters at your back – at least with this viking Gael, he cannot get away with plotting openly if you can understand just some of his Gaelic. The rest will be spread over. We'd be foolish to group them up on one farm. Go on, Eirik, take your thrall, he owns a cat – yours now, too."

Eirik climbed up the ladder up to the ship. Asgeir met his gaze, nonplussed.

"I am Eirik Blackhead, herse to the Jarl. My farm is well-stocked and I have many thralls – and they are well fed. Listen to me and you will be treated right. I know you understand Norse."

"I have nothing to say to you. I am no thrall."

Éabhín, your tongue lashed anyone who dared call you one. I'll honor you by doing much of the same.

"Both Gaels and Nordmenn know that when Father War humbles men, they live on as chattel," Eirik said. "Accept what has been spun for you, it will be easier."

"I accept that I am of Odin's kin, when he guised as Jarl, not Eirik, and certainly not Thrall. When he helped the three kins of man upon Midgard, my bloodline sprung from Jarl's seed."

Eirik gestured to his Pictish servants.

"Unchain him, but keep your wits about you."

Asgeir turned to the wordless sailors.

"You shouldn't be seeing them again, and come summer, they will be scattered throughout all lands of Nordmenn like unguarded sheep, but if that's your farewell, I'll allow it." Eirik said.

Asgeir refused to budge as the Picts tugged upon his chain. The pointy-bearded one brandished a birch club. "Move it."

"Hit me then."

The Pict raised his weapon to strike; cracks veined, and Asgeir just stared him down. Eirik waved his hand and knocked the club away.

"He will learn his place in time, Earp."

"My place is on the battlefield, Eirik," Asgeir said. "I proved myself at the Battle of Borgund. I survived that even with a spear to the chest, and I swam to shore after the wreck of the Sea-Bitch. I've not lost my heart like the other unfortunate sailors, but you'll find it granite."

"All men's hearts are soapstone," Eirik said, "that's what my father told me. You'll learn what that means in time."

Down in a small boat, the Picts rowed in the choppy sea toward a bay. Asgeir sought to free himself: a whack of the oar, the seizure of the Pict's club, or to wrap his elbow around Eirik's neck. But he found no reason for quarrel when outnumbered, and nothing but Aegir's watery daughters under him. Eirik shaded his eyes from the dawning sun and spoke to Asgeir.

"It's been hard on the Orkneys lately. Jarl Toke's missing, and I pray to Red Thor that he lives. Much of our crops failed before last winter, and our harvest was light. We're lucky to have enough fodder for the beasts."

Asgeir turned his head and looked westward. *Father, I will find you. I'll never submit to thralldom.*

"You work for a few years, maybe I will free you," Eirik said, and Earp cast a glance over his shoulder as he rowed. "You're a Nordmann, son of Rig.

Just follow orders and I'll treat you as a good thrall, as I am sure you treated your good thralls back in Norway."

After they rowed for several hours, passing by small, flat islands peopled with farms and sheep, they headed eastward toward a sandy bay, where half-finished boathouses stretched into the foamy waters. Upon the ridgeline at the brink where beach met plowed field, a stone-walled hall lay, boat-shaped, with an overturned ship upon it, its hull the roof. It all sat upon a mound of green, with tumbledown of hewn-square stones down into the shores below.

At late afternoon, there at high tide, the vessel boat glided into the naust. They disembarked, and the Picts dragged the boat inside.

"We're building Jarl Toke a hall," Eirik said, and gestured to Earp.

Earp had small, dark eyes that eyes that never ceased to squint. His bottom lip jutted outward, blemished white, and blue blotches pocked his teeth.

"See those stones?" Earp pointed toward the tumbledown from the mound. "The ones cut?"

Asgeir said nothing but Earp continued.

"They are not to be touched."

"Why not?" Asgeir asked.

"I'm the slave master, and I am not to be questioned."

"Why not?" Asgeir said again with a grin.

Earp's face darkened uglier. "What did I just say?"

"I am curious," Asgeir said, "would you deny a man knowledge?"

"Let him alone, Earp," Eirik said. "Asgeir – take a nap if you need it. It's been a long day for you," he said, and left, met by two raven-haired girls in undyed smocks near the entrance to the hull-roofed hall.

"I shall nap," Asgeir said, "because I am very tired, not because you allowed me."

Eirik laughed, and he and Earp met eyes. "Don't worry, Earp, he'll get used to it in due time."

"Master Eirik," Earp said, but Eirik turned heel and walked up the trackway.

Asgeir followed him up, and glanced over his shoulder to find Earp there at the foamy shoreline, dour-faced among the other thralls.

"You'll find your quarters there," Eirik said and pointed toward a simple hut some hundred paces from the would-be-hall. "Find a thrall to show you your bed – and no lusty glances at my sisters. Now, I bid you farewell."

Asgeir found himself midway up the track, and each step heavier than the last. The weight of the day hung on him, and his eyes bleared in the dimlight of the island. From a collapsed hillside, some hewn blocks spilled out. Among the ashy soil, he found chips of pottery, shells, and rusted nails. An old house. A Pictish house?

He bent over and snatched up a small block, hand-sized, and walked up the trackway. *Order me around, you ugly thrall?* Near the Jarl's new hall, he found a pile of worked stone. He placed the rubble stone there among the pile, and then found his quarters. A young girl with a wide smile pointed toward a bed of straw, and after he gathered some for a pillow, found sleep.

Asgeir drew Gael-Kisser from its scabbard and awaited the duel to the death. The sun gleamed off his sword's blade, sheened nearly white. He stepped over the furrow in the ground that marked the dueling-circle. His enemy approached him with his sword revved in his veined hand.

Ulf the Old stood at-the-ready in his silver chainmail hauberk. His leathery, sea-bitten face grinned as he walked alongside toward the circle. A pointed helmet capped his head, with a nosepiece over his face, and its aventail shuffled behind his shoulders. He wore his yellow tunic underneath, vibrant tansy dyed, with brown britches tucked into his madder-red winnigas that ran ankle to knee. In his hand, a shield, white-faced and yellow-stripped, the sigil of his sail and crew of the Sea-Bitch.

The ship rocked, moored just beyond the sands. The brink of her portside was covered in Ulf's warriors, beating their yellow-striped shields with their spearshafts.

"Ulf!" they chanted. "Ulf! Ulf!"

Chief among them stood Rolf Ulfsson, the son of Ulf the Old. "My friend," he said to Asgeir, "it's been so long!" he shouted, but his shout muffled under the chant.

Asgeir readied the sword in his hand. Each of his fingers held the leathery grip, and he slid his thumb over the bronze-plated crossguard and onto the flat of the underside of the blade. Just as his father taught him to hold the sword, so he may dip and pry and crack the tip like a whip against his enemy.

Ulf stepped over the rope and centered himself in the ring. He outstretched his arm, widened his legs, and leaned forward.

Alongside the warriors on the ship stood Njall Gray-haired, tip-toed to peer over the shoulders of the taller warriors in front of him. "Come on, Asgeir! He's lanky but you're average. You know what to do!"

Éabhín approached him now, her thick red hair plaited under a silk kerchief. She wore a piebald green, red, and blue cloak wrapped many times around her body, over a lichen-dyed purple dress. Her bare feet stepped gingerly at the threshold of the ring. She carried a shield wrong-side-out in her underarm. With a curtsy, she handed it to him.

Yellow stripes painted over a white background. Asgeir stood puzzled at it for a spell. "Ulf's shield? I'm not in Ulf's crew. I am here to slay Ulf, to avenge my brother Odd, with my father's sword!"

A seagull wheeled overhead. The messenger of Njordr, god of the sea, of sailors, of merchants. Not a god of duels or single combat or honor. Why?

"Arrogance," Ulf said as he lunged forward, sword-point first. In an eyeblink, Asgeir found himself back on Holm, over his ashen brother, lapped at by the cold tide.

"The snap of a whip," Njall said, his feet on the gunwale. "Use your wrist! I taught you that!"

Something cracked. Asgeir woke up.

"Your nap is over, now get to work," a husky voice said. Something snapped on the wall behind him.

Asgeir woke and found himself gazing outside at the greensward. A flock of sheep bleated, strewn around the brown hill like ripe dandelions. He shivered in the cold Westwind that shocked him with sleet sideways. He dragged his thick woolen hood over his head as he drunk-walked toward the door.

"Hurry up with those legs," the whip-hand said. It was brawny Earp. He wore a thick brown cloak over most of his body.

"I can't shake off my tiredness," Asgeir said.

"I said hurry up with those legs, or they'll be fettered."

That Eirik will acknowledge my kinship. I'll not last a thrall for long. Father always said to never surrender to thralldom if ever captured in battle. I will honor him, and it will free me.

The whip cracked and Asgeir lurched forward. Pain splashed across his back, the wool of his tunic tore. He caught himself and crouched.

"I said, get up and get to work!"

The whip cracked again and Asgeir slammed to the soggy ground. He reeled there, blood trickled from his browridge and clouded the sight in his right eye.

"Master allowed you to keep your cat, yet you disobey us? Master will hear about this," Earp said. He whistled.

Two other thralls, wolf-lean boys, trotted over both leftward and rightward to him. They each held Asgeir's arms. Asgeir budged and twisted wild but they held tight as the overseer approached him with a roll of heather twine.

With much knotwork, they tied Asgeir's hands behind his back. The thrall duo dragged him across the wet, cold pasture and toward a small shack.

"Unruly slaves get beatings," Earp said. "We will beat order into your chaos."A balled fist struck him. His head reeled back and he stumbled. The thralls held him up as the brawny Pict punched Asgeir in the belly, his hairy fist plunged into Asgeir's hard, heaving stomach so that he almost spewed. A second punch drilled into his chest, and the wind squeezed out of his lungs. Asgeir reeled when the Pict kicked heel-first into his thigh.

He gulped in his breath and found the surly Pict akimbo, straight-backed and smiling.

The world wheeled around him. Lights pinioned. He found blackness.

In dreamland, a mound struck against the sky on the otherwise flat land. Low-cut grass swayed in the wind as Asgeir started toward it. It stood three men high, he reckoned, and broadwise, three horses long. In the rosy-fingered dawn, he circled it. Facing westward, he found the gangway.

Two posts upheld a tunnel that led inside. He walked in, the red-orange light dappled inside to light it.

The lich of Ulf sprawled out spreadeagled in the grave. It wore a fine tunic as blue as his mother's eyes. His head rested on a shield, yellow-striped and white-backed. On his right shoulder, he held a sword abreast. The stance of the defender.

Asgeir crept closer, and the eyes of the lifeless man opened. Steely-blue as the choppy sea. He sat up and walked toward him, sword on his shoulder.

The afterwalker!

"You're dead," he said.

"I am the afterwalker," it said.

"You're in Ran's realm."

"It's too cold down there," it said with a sneer. "Now, move away so I may leave."

"Where are you going?" Asgeir asked. "Lie back down and rest."

"I have no mound for I drowned at sea," it said with a retch. "Therefore, I am the afterwalker. Your aunt hexed me to be this way."

"Hex or not, your ship hit dryrocks."

"She hexed us. The Sea-Bitch is sunk. Many of her sailors litter the seabed. Njall is dead. Rolf is fatherless. You're a thrall. It's the volva's fault."

The afterwalker shuffled up from its resting place. Rusted iron rivets crumbled into dust as it slid upon its unsteady legs and stepped forward. Asgeir evaded its shambling stride, backed against the frigid wall of the mound as the afterwalker lurched for the out-way.

Without any other pathways, Asgeir left the mound. Once he reached the shimmering outside, he turned and found that the afterwalker held his father's sword.

A hex on my lips,

To Ran with your ship.

The bane of Auntie Bjørg woke him.

Asgeir found himself in a dank cowshed, hogtied, splattered in cowpies. He peaked out through cracks in the planks.

I am no thrall. I am no slave. He thought of Éabhín, and how she refused those words. *That Irish lass, I wonder how she fares?*

My forebears watch me. My gods look over me. That Eirik will come to his senses, once he understands who I am.

The door swung open and daylight spilled into the shed. Earp stormed, club in one fist, and the other balled. He dragged Asgeir upright and raised the weapon overhead. Behind him, more thralls crowded into the shed in twos and threes.

The must of sweat overcame the dung pile as throngs of thralls of all ages stood in every cranny of the cowshed, and all faced him. The two wolf-lean thralls held whips as they urged the other thralls on to watch.

"The thrall will work," Earp said.

Yesterday, defeated. Today, bedraggled in a cowshed. Tomorrow, surely Hel-ward, for he would die heart unshackled, or join them as a warrior, akin to his blood.

"Where is your master?" Asgeir asked.

"That's not your concern," Earp said and waved the club sunwise around Asgeir's head.

"Who will tell him that you bashed the skull of the son of the Hallgeir of Lothlend?"

The Pictish man laughed.

"Not the club, yet. You can just agree to get to work. If not, the whip."

"I am no thrall, my grandfather lies in the mound of my farm, sword in hand, horse at feet."

"I'll have you know my grandfather lies on this land, under the green earth, before..."

"Before the Nordmenn came?" Asgeir asked with a choke. Rubies of blood had been splashed about his face.

"Do you agree," Earp said through his teeth, "to work or not?"

"I'm not a thrall," Asgeir said, "beat me to death if you must, but know that my father will avenge me with your head."

The thralls murmured behind Earp. Asgeir wrenched about in his binds, for the lash left three stings, but he shoved his bound feet into the muck underneath him, clenched his teeth, and spoke.

"Your grandfather lays under green earth, does he gaze up at you in pride? Or does he stir in his grave that you beat a bound man?"

Earp huffed, cursed blackly in his tongue, balled a fist, and punched the ground. He raised the whip, its warm leather strip braised the jutted chin of Asgeir. But the overseer failed to strike.

"Refusal to work," he said, then spoke Pictish to one of the thralls, an older man with a hunched back. That thrall scurried out.

"There is fodder to be gathered, there are baskets to be woven, roofs to fix, cows to milk, butter to churn."

"Let me serve as a fighter," Asgeir said, "thralldom is not fit for my blood, a landed free man."

"Is that so?" Earp asked. The whip cracked twice crosswise on Asgeir's chest. He jumped up and down to stifle a scream.

The hunchbacked man returned with something squirming in his arms.

"Cat," he said in his tongue, "here you go."

Earp held a black furry cat by the scruff in his left hand. He brandished it at Asgeir. The cat wiggled but otherwise stayed tame. *Svartganger*!

"Get to work, or I'll kill it."

Asgeir choked. "He's not yours to decide that."

"Get to work, or it'll be skinned, and I'll wipe my arse with its hide."

"He's not yours to do that. What would your master say if you did that to his mouser?"

The yellow eyes of Svartganger darted, and he meowed and writhed hard in the dirty hand of the Pict.

"You wouldn't kill a cat, would you?" Asgeir said.

"I wouldn't?"

"And what say the rest of you?" Asgeir said to the nine thralls. "Do you want him dead?"

"How will I kill him?" the Pict asked. "A firebrand? Some hot oil?"

"You will ruin the master's stuffs?" Asgeir said but the Pict just grinned wider.

"Your last chance to spare the life of the cat. Swear your fealty to me, your overseer, to work, to obey my word, to follow my orders, to..."

The door of the cowshed opened. All the thralls turned and there Eirik stood, a thick yellow cloak over brown trousers with high boots. He unhooded himself and shook water out of his hair like a dog.

"Why are you all in here?" he asked and spotted Asgeir, slumped against the backside of the cowshed.

"What did he do?"

"Nothing, Master Eirik," Earp said. "He refuses to work."

"Refuses to work? And what are you doing to that cat? Put him down!"

Earp dropped Svartganger, and he scampered away and out of the cowshed.

"All of you, leave – now."

The thralls left the cowshed, one by one, the door waved in the wind, Earp glowered at Asgeir and left, then Eirik shut the door and approached him.

Eirik placed a mittened hand on the quivering face of Asgeir.

"What misdeed have you done?"

"I refused to work."

"Why?"

"I'm not a thrall."

"Man, you're already beaten," he said. "and I see that stitched-up wound on you, too. Looks like Orkney wasn't your first time going a'viking."

"I earned that spear wound defending Jarl Haakon of Borgund's hall from an invader," Asgeir said. "I fought with honor and I will die with honor."

"You were sold to me as a thrall, not a viking," he said, and his smile widened.

"I am from Jarl," Asgeir said.

"And sometimes, the Norns spin cruelty, when Jarl-blooded men are forced into thralldom."

"But I'm highborn."

"Don't whine at your fate. Reject your lament. Holdfast against dread."

"My father is the huskarl to the King of Lothlend."

Eirik's smile faded. "The Norns are cruel indeed."

"You must let me go," Asgeir said with a wince as his wounds grew stingier.

"I must not do anything you ask of me, thrall."

"My father will demand it."

"He will have to parley, just like anyone else. Neither the huskarl nor the King of Lothlend himself say in the matters of Orkney. That's the Jarl's wisdom."

Asgeir went silent for a spell, and looked upon his chest and belly. It had been mangled in lashes, and worse, one tore open his old spear wound from back at the Battle of Borgund. That battle, his first foray in the battleline, the din of iron and wood and bone. He fought with bravery, but he hadn't the skill to avoid the spearhead that, by Thor's defending hand, had stayed from his liver or heart. He still worried of fester, a graver danger now. And there was no Saga the Healer to sew him up now.

"If your father is who you say he is, then I ought to free you from thralldom, since I want no ill will with Lothlend. But you will work for me still."

Eirik reached for a knife that hung in a sheath from his belt. He unsheathed it and cut Asgeir's bonds. Asgeir slunk down among the muck, rose to his feet, and stood face to face with him.

"Come, we'll clean and stitch you. And clothe you. And your sword will be given back to you. You'll serve me as a watchman until summer."

Relief soothed over Asgeir. "No sense in tempting Aegir's daughters this late in the year – I will leave come summer, when the weather is fair, and find my father in the South Isles."

I'm no slave, Odin, I am your son, I am Hallgeir's son, and I will live and die as one. Maybe the sea did make me a man, Ulf. And someday, I'll have a crew like yours.

CHAPTER IV

The Watchman

The waves lapped over the sandy mound just at the shoreline. Asgeir walked around it sunwise, his patchy yellow cloak rippling in the wind behind him, under an ochre-colored shield slung over his back, the colors of Jarl Toke. He watched the seas from the hill that overlooked the farm. The days, weeks, and months passed as Asgeir overwintered on the island of Rousay. Yule, the holiest of days, went with a meager feast. The new year roared in with such foul wind and rain that he often sat drenched, waiting and watching for the dumbest and luckiest enemies that would dare sail in that weather. When it all warmed and the thralls tilled the fields and planted seeds, Asgeir welcomed it, but none had heard news of Jarl Toke.

Svartganger stalked the fallowed fields as Asgeir watched the first merchant ships of the year sail into the darkening island-group. Each day, he marched up and down and to and fro as he scanned the choppy sound for vikings. Each night, he dreamed of the afterwalker, soundless, beckoning him to lay there in the mound, maggots flowing from his rotten yellow teeth. That nightmare lurked nightly and he came to dread sleeping.

The morning bit into him as cold as the Westwind. He tried to finger the silver brooch at his collar, but found nothing but a bone-pin. The brooch, his cloak, his clothes, his shield – all at the bottom of some bay.

The Sea-Bitch, with its dragon-headed prow, and proud sail piped in wind. They braved the storm and in the face of defeat, the sailors stroked on through the open sea, with neither bird nor star to guide their course. Most dead and gone. Let me alone, afterwalker. I wait for winter's end, so I may find my father again, and fight alongside him. I yearn for that, and I will no longer dwell in the past.

Asgeir walked alongshore as those waves eased, and the thralls waded out waist-deep into the sea, where they piled up pylons to build a boathouse for Jarl Toke.

He found himself lonely on that wave-crashed bay, so he followed the cattle-trail up into the hills. From the vantage of the highest crest, he could scan the waterways for unwelcome ships. The fog had cleared by midday, and he watched the seas until it started to haze the horizon again.

That mist, where Thor cracked his hammer back in Norway when the Sea-Bitch set sail for its final journey.

But I am no slave, and I even have friends in Orkney. Rolf, he lives on, and I wonder how he fares. But what must Rolf think? His father is dead. My poor friend! What awful news. And how could I face him, part rests upon me, and my aunt's hex.

Odd's valkyrie-searching eyes stared glassy, skyward. *And I must tell my father of his death, too.*

Asgeir approached the old cairn there on the mountaintop. "I need the gods to answer me, for no one here on Midgard can."

The loch up there, a span of black water mirror-shone, stood quiet. He reached into his wool satchel, broke off a piece of flatbread, and tossed it into the water.

"To the elves of the land," he said. "Guide me, and guard me, while I am so far from home."

Something peeped up from beyond a hillock to his right-side. A small chuckle. Two black-haired shapes ducked under the heather.

He strode over the hill, and there found a standing-stone, a *bautstein*, an upright slab, flat struck against the overcast sky. Some giggling fluttered up behind him. He turned his head, and two white faces peeked out from the other side of the stone, and then back.

Eirik's two sisters kneeled on the soggy ground by the base of the stone. An array of herbs, buds, and berries lay between them. They both looked about as many winters as he, with simple brown dresses, and barefoot despite the coldness of the ground. They had black hair covered in wool hoods.

"You thought we were sidhe," the eldest said, using the Gaelic word for elves "It's me, Drusticca – and Fina!" the same girl said.

"We've just offered to the sidhe, and we heard you offering to them. It's surely right that you found us now. Maybe you'd join us?" Drusticca asked.

"I offered to the elves, not the sidhe," he said.

"They're the same!" said Fina. Her brown eyes looked large and warm, and in the dimness of the foggy hills, flecks of green pocked them, lichen-like.

Their eyes reminded them of Sakka's. She had been his lover for an evening when he had been taken hostage by Arild, who wished to avenge an insult spewed by Ulf. Madness grasped hold of Arild, and drove him to murder Asgeir and the crew. Sakka, his bride-to-be, chose Asgeir over the berserker. She was a Finngirl, whose father wished to avenge her deflowering, and her fate a mystery after the Jarl Haakon defeated them at Borgund. For an eyeblink, her white, lithe, quivering nude body flashed in his mind. *My love, Sakka.*

"We call them elves in Norway," Asgeir said.

"You're another Nordmann?"

"I'm from Eigg, in the South Isles."

"The Hebrides! Our cousins lived there, before the heathens came across the sea," Drusticca said.

"Well, my mother is from Ireland, my father Norway, and I was raised in Hordaland."

"Then what are you?" Drusticca asked and squinted her eyes.

"Well, the elves are called sidhe by you, right?"

"Aye," Drusticca said, not ceasing to squint.

"I suppose they call me the Viking Gael, so that is what I am," he said. "But aren't you girls Picts? You worship the White Christ."

"Aye," Drusticca said. "But we still love our sidhe. When White Christ died, all the sidhe wept."

"Then what are you?" he asked them.

They looked at each other, both grinning as if he should know the answer.

"We were here long before the Northmen," Drusticca said. "We will always be us, and not you, no matter what our brother, now called Eirik Blackhead, says… but come, the weather changes."

A blackness clouded the western horizon. Asgeir followed the two girls away from the hill and back down to the farm. It drizzled, spat, then rained. Asgeir draped himself in his cloak, and the two girls donned their hoods. As Drusticca turned to leave, Fina slunk away from her sister.

"It's that special time of day," she said. "I'll show you what we are."

She hurried down the sward from the hill to the seashore. The current brought in hefty waves, rolling like carts in race. "Come on, before Earp notices I'm gone!"

He chased after her, down to where the cattle grazed on the kelp smattered across the rocky beach. They followed the shoreline, her bare feet gingerly pacing through craggy, slippery rocks. When they got so far down shore that the hall on the hillock and all of its thrall-buildings had been shrouded in mist, she stopped him. She stood on a rock to be as tall as him, and with a hand dripping in beads of water, pointed seaward.

A black bulbous head poked up from the surface. A seal. It turned its head and vanished into the depths.

"We're from the seals," she said. "They were our alderelders. The selkie, the seal that shapeshifts into a man or woman, and one shared the bed of the first Pictish King."

She waved in the seal's direction with a wry smile. "I come out here when there's mist, so Earp can't see me stole away. He doesn't like me talking to the seals."

"Why do you talk to seals?"

"They listen," she said with a giggle. "Earp thinks it's foolish."

"What's it to him?"

"He's a Christian," she said, "I mean, so am I. But ever since you, the heathens, came along, they don't like that we sacrifice to the sidhe, or to seals."

"But Eirik is no Christian."

"Nay," Fina said, "he's taken up the Heathen faith – so he's forsaken Christ, and worships Thor, Freya, Freyr, and all your other gods. Just like he's taken up the name Eirik. But in the end, he'll be buried in our family graveyard, Heathen or not."

"I don't understand," Asgeir said, "what's wrong with worshipping White Christ and Red Thor? The elves and the sidhe? The saints and the selkies?"

Fina looked over his shoulder, and darted her eyes around, even spying behind a boulder to see if anyone had followed them.

"White Christ and his father do not welcome those in the afterlife that offer to other gods. But for me, Asgeir, I don't know. When I pray to the sidhe and the selkies, they answer me. When I pray to the Callieach, the hag of winter, she blesses our heifers with milk. I never get anything from White Christ."

"The gods come to me in dreams," Asgeir said in an undertone.

She placed a soft hand on his wet chest. "You can say what you want, as loud as you want, because you are free," she raised her voice. "So speak louder! Let all hear how Asgeir of Eigg speaks to the gods in his dreams!"

She bowled over laughing. "Oh no," she said and turned back to the sea, now bare of beasts. "Where's the seal? I scared him away."

"If the rumble of those waves doesn't scare him away, then nothing will. I suppose it's no use keeping it secret. Ullr, the God of hunts, duels, wild – he came to me and told me the skill that I needed to win a duel. I did so, but it was the same skill that slew my brother days prior."

Fina bit her lip. "Slew your brother?"

"Yes. An old viking came to collect the debts he swore my father owed him. We refused. We dueled him and his son, and we lost, when my brother got a sword through the eye."

She snarled. In one fell swoop, she ripped a jagged piece of slate off the ground and jutted it into the air. "If anyone hurt one of my siblings – I'd stab them! Stab them to death!"

"He's… he drowned," he said, "Njordr came to me in a dream, and told me that our ship. Well, his ship, the Sea-Bitch, will sink. The ship sank. Just a handful of his sailors survived. And now I am here, with my cat."

Fina nodded. "I'm glad you live, and that cat is cute. But the gods come to you in your dreams."

"I thought I was to die," he said, and found his wound itched. The drunkenness of battle overcame him for a spell, and he shivered, in both fear and awe. "I found myself in Valhal, where…"

"Where only the bravest warriors go. Where the valkyries fly and bring them up and there's mead and forever-fights. Yes, I know. Eirik talks about it all the time."

"He's a warrior then," Asgeir said.

"That's why he gave himself over to Odin. He scares me, yet enthralls me. He's the grim-one, a mask… masks are terrifying. I am much like Freya. If I were a Heathen, I would pay tribute to her," she said and threw her hair over her shoulder. "I am a maiden, after all, and I'll never fall for Earp's courting," she said and winked.

Eirik forbid lusty glances at his sisters, but Fina reminds me of Sakka. It's risky to be alone with her now, but if it pisses Earp off, then I care not.

"Has Odin ever come to you in a dream?"

"In Valhal, his hall, despite that I never call upon him, because he is a terrible God, though we love him, he is the bringer of storms. War. One does not call upon him lightly."

"Well," Fina said as she looked over both her shoulders to ensure no one heard, "I think he is real, and he likes to make war."

"I don't think he likes it much," Asgeir said, "I think he thinks war is needed."

"Why would it be needed?"

"We don't know," Asgeir said.

"He is many steps ahead, like a game of hnefatafl. To save the king, one must sometimes sacrifice his men."

"So he does sacrifice men, as the monks claim!" Fina said with her arms akimbo.

"In war, yes," Asgeir said. "Only the bravest men are chosen by him."

Fina's eyes went wide. "Do you want that, Asgeir?"

That took him aback.

"What son of Odin wouldn't? If he deems one honorable enough, then hardly a man would say no."

"But I know of Valhal," she said, "that is where Odin's chosen go. They fight and die in pain daily! That is why the Christian paradise is better."

"What's the Christian paradise?" Asgeir asked.

"Happiness forever!" she said and threw her arms heavenward. "No pain, no hunger, no violence. I'd like you there with me, Asgeir."

Asgeir attempted to fathom that. He thought of his pig on the old farm, happily scarfing up scraps in its pen before slaughter, without worry, without pain, without hunger, without violence, only happiness, in Christian heaven.

"I'm no pig," Asgeir said, "and your paradise sounds like a pigpen."

Fina placed a hand over her mouth, and grasped his wrist with the other. "Blasphemy! Asgeir, how could you say such a thing to me! We broke bread at Yule!"

Asgeir turned toward the sea and gazed westward. The wind and rain whipped him in the face. *Thor, I am your friend. Let me fight in battle as my father does. And if I am ever deemed worthy of your respect, tell your father to invite me into Valhal.*

Fina put her hands on his shoulders. He returned to Midgard then. "Why would you say that?" she asked.

"I want Valhal, and we will say farewell before the afterlife, come summer," he said with a smile.

She looked up at him, wet-eyed, and blinked. "But who is going to look out for me and Drusticca?"

"I've evaded my duty long enough," he said.

"And that would upset my brother, would it? You can spend time with me, away from him, and that ugly thrall Earp, who seldom leaves me be, I just want to be away from them for a while," she said, big-eyed, face wet from rain, drenched hair coiled. She grabbed him by the neck and kissed him.

He held her for lip's embrace, but pulled back.

Is she trying to trouble me with Earp or Eirik?

She laughed. "Earp would be enraged in jealousy if he witnessed that! Oh, I could kiss you all day, knowing that it would make him squirm! And Eirik would be sour, too."

Over the waves, a spikey, malformed shape glide shoreward.

Fina turned and gasped. "That's a longship!"

Asgeir and Fina raced down the shore, and found a colorless sail flapping hard in the heavy wind.

"That looks like a warship!" Asgeir said, and Fina looked aghast.

"Harald's men?" Fina asked.

"I don't know – go alert Eirik!"

"No, he'll have me hide. I will fight," she said, whipped her satchel around her waist, and pulled out a flint-bladed knife.

"A knife when they have spears?" Asgeir asked as the ship fast-approached, lightning-swift toward the landing-place between the headland and farm. He wrung his face troll-like and shouted at her, "Now!"

Fina's mouth gaped and she dashed away, and vanished into the creeping mist of the moor.

Asgeir wrapped his hand around the leathered hilt of Gael-Kisser as he sped toward the landing-place. An answer from Odin, of all gods?

Eighteen oarsmen rowed the nimble craft to the bay through shore-waves. They spotted Asgeir first, and a man at the prow, a young man with curly blond hair, but a long mustache, hailed him. *Vikings. I will stand my ground, as my duty, and my honor demands it.*

Asgeir stood as the gateway to Toke's farm. The thralls must have alerted Eirik, but these men were going viking. Their colorless sail flailed in the wind as the western wind-hammer struck, and the ship jutted away from the coast but the sternboardside rowed hard, and they beached there near the old round cairn and tombs of the Picts.

Their captain furled up a hemp ladder, and the vikings clambered down to the strand, one by one. A small band of just eighteen, they wore ragged, threadbare tunics. backstepped several paces from them.

The prow of the ship hit the beachhead, and Asgeir found himself small in front of its great wooden breast, as Freyr against the fire giant Surtr.

"Hail, watchman of Toke. I am Tormod the Colorless."

"What is your business at Jarl Toke's farm?" Asgeir asked, but knew. The eighteen sea-wolves had hungry blades in their hands.

"The Jarl is missing and we are hungry. Step aside," Tomor said and threw his long blond hair over his shoulder. "We will plunder the farm, and leave you unharmed." He had a short chin and arced his damp hair from his youthful face, and he slapped the haft of his sheathed axe. "Move along and you go unscathed. I can tell by your twang you are from Hordaland. So we are kin. I hail from Voss."

"I am Asgeir, and I am tasked to defend this farm against raids. I stand against you, kinsman or not."

The men that stood before him all wielded spears and axes, and many shields, all painted with oxblood. The eighteen vikings disembarked and colored the strand in red and rusty iron.

"By good Thor, we have no wish to kill you," Tormod said.

"I may have a wish to kill you."

Tormod stiffened, and his oarsmen balked at that, and some readied their spears.

"I am the son of Hallgeir," Asgeir said.

"The huskarl to Lothlend? By Thor, I didn't expect his son here! Just what are you doing in Orkney? Never mind that – step aside. We came here for a fight against Toke's men, not the son of Hallgeir. Step down," Tormod said and drew his axe. He tore the sheath off to show a nicked edge. "Or I'll put you down."

With a step backward, Asgeir drew his sword, the Gael-Kisser, in a rasp. He trembled as violence hung in the air, harsher than the wind, colder than the seawater, and bleaker than the sky. But the leathered grip of Gael-Kisser, his father's sword, soothed him. *This is not my fight, blast it, but I must follow my word.*

Tormod paced himself from Asgeir. He stood under the prow of his ship, its hull clad in barnacles, its rigging ropes frayed. He looked wolfish, as did the vikings that circled him and Asgeir now. Hungry eyes all on Asgeir.

"To best the son of Lothlend in a duel," Tormod said, "would bring fame to me. I will make quick work of you, and then we will fill our coffers."

"If I win, you leave this farm unmolested," Asgeir said.

Sweat and coldness. Each wave sent a shiver into him. Beyond Tormod, the Pictish graveyard jutted out into the ocean. The sea would lap at it until skeletons slipped out and the bone-gnawers had much feasting. Would Eirik bury him there if he died on the strand, died in battle, holding his word as stubborn as a badger in its den?

No, I fight, I'm the son of the huskarl to the King of Lothlend. I wield my father's sword. I will best this viking.

"Ullr, God of duels, guide me," Asgeir said as he and Tormod approached each other. They both unhooked the shields strapped to their backs and, now sword-and-board, the duel formed.

"Ullr decides who is the bravest," Tormod said. "And that is me."

"Arrogance," Ulf's nonplussed voice chimed in Asgeir's head.

Tormod swept back his heavy brown cloak to reveal a patchwork tunic. He peered over Asgeir's head. The latter shot a glance over his shoulder and found a host of men that crested the hill. Soon, stragglers gathered. Two young men loped from the hinterlands, both spear-armed, and Eirik rushed out from the mead-hall, his cloak waved as he led the burgeoned nine-strong band shoreward.

Tormod raised his shield, much paint-chipped, with a frayed rawhide rim, and a bashed-in iron boss.

Before Asgeir could signal to them, Tormod thrust forward, axe-first. Asgeir raised his sword, parried so the axe-edge rang against the flat of his blade, and flipped the other edge for a head cut. Tormod sidestepped and flung his axe at Asgeir, who jumped out of the way. Tormod spat to the side and each of them eyed the other.

Tormod war-danced, his wrist flowing the axe upward, downward, rightward, leftward in arcs, and when Asgeir stepped forward to slash at his leg, the paint-chipped shield smashed into his face as the crowd of warriors reacted in a loud roar.

Midgard spun, the ground blued, and the sky browned. Asgeir found himself crumpled to his knees as he blinked the sparks away, and tasted copper. Blood streamed from his face.

In an eyeblink, Tormod had gripped his hair and held his axe aloft as if to cleave his skull in twain. Asgeir gazed beyond the red-faced, heaving viking and beyond to the slither of blue in the sky. Valhal.

"I defeated you," he said, and released Asgeir.

"Take his sword," one of the vikings said.

"No," Tormod said as everything blurred for Asgeir. "Else the Gael-Slayer will venge upon us."

"Helvete," Asgeir said as he staggered drunkenly to his feet. He tried to gather his bearings, scattered about like a broken pot.

Tormod charged upslope along with his vikings, armed with spears and axes. Asgeir's sight focused, his wit whet, and he found the vikings' assault met by a bulwark of Eirik and his men. Eirik leapt off his horse and the riderless steed raced away as he led the countercharge. They clashed in a din of iron and wood and the tramp of feet in the fallowed field.

Asgeir shook himself back to Midgard as the battle flashed. A viking groaned with a javelin stuck out of his gizzard, and he flopped over and broke the shaft underneath him. The line of eighteen broadened to attempt to flank the defenders on both ends. Eirik shouted from behind his large ochre-painted shield to halt that, as their line stretched thin.

Asgeir raced up the slope, keeping range from the vikings, and wheeled around the battlelines to join Eirik's. He brandished Gael-Kisser, a hard clang rattled from afar, over the slope.

"I've lost again in a duel," he said to himself. "I'll not lose next time."

Asgeir flew up the trackway, his face as red as a viking's blade, his eyes searing Tormod in the battle. The viking on the outmost flank pivoted and cast a javelin at him. He nearly shat himself as he landed upon his belly. The tanged blade sank into the ground just a fingerbreadth from his leg. He got up and yanked it in one fell swoop and ran, zigzagged up the hill to thwart more javelins from being cast at him, and reached the rear of the line.

With his tongue pressed to the roof of his mouth, Asgeir chucked the javelin over the heavy-shielded men at Tormod. The viking captain raised his shield and blocked, the point checked off its iron shield boss, and his comrade kicked it back. A javelin crashed through the shield of a boy no older than thirteen winters, and he cried and limped out of the line. As Asgeir approached the fray, his heart raced as both sides waited, just out of spear's reach, quaking hands on spearshafts and axe hafts and knife handles.

The boy staggered past Asgeir as he stepped in line, and Eirik shouted at him.

"To the right flank!"

Asgeir trotted to where three wiry young men all armed with axes and shields pulsed forward. The trio kicked up mud as they charged, but they had feigned, for they halted and backed away as the right flank of the defenders bowed forward, the left flank of the enemies stretched.

Outflanked, Eirik's leftmost warrior took a spear stab to the ribs. He crumbled to the ground in a silent heap as the vikings were upon them.

A bloody, severed hand bounced off Asgeir's leg as he found three spears aimed at him. Eirik shouted above all, unarmed, hands over his head.

"Mercy!"

Tormod shouted as he raised his axe skyward.

"To Odin, victory!"

The vikings all cheered and beat their spearshafts against their shields in a din, and they tramped about in a whirlwind of sand on the beach. Back at the farm, Drusticca and Fina ducked behind a pair of barrels, and fled into the open door of the mead-hall.

"You won," Eirik said, "name your price."

"We'll be taking your foodstuffs," Tormod said, "and for my prize, my sore eyes have a sight already."

I told you to hide, Fina! As watchman, he'll take them over my battered body.

Asgeir shoved the nearest spear by its shaft and charged the closest enemy, a spearman. The stench of the sweaty foeman and his raspy, heaving voice faded when Asgeir shouldered him. Wet sticky flesh met as the spearman slammed to the ground and Asgeir jumped over him. He rushed toward the mead-hall as Eirik shouted.

"Asgeir, come back! Stop, or they will kill you!"

No, I will not. I will not let them take Fina and Drusticca. I'll die with honor, and haunt them like an afterwalker.

Asgeir ran as fast as when Loki raced living fire, stepping around a cairn, clambered over a short fence, and started right for the mead-hall. Just as he ran past the cowshed, someone burst out from around its corner.

Earp was upon Asgeir. The must of him, the slime of his shirtless body, his short arms untamable. Asgeir found himself on his arse as the Pict punched him in the head, rock-like, his neck strained, and he raised his arms to defend himself, but dirty, blistered knuckles crashed through his palms and rattled his head. His ears rang and he stumbled up again, dazed, tripped back down, and the Pict dragged him by the feet down the hill.

"Here you are, I bring you this rascal, Asgeir," the Pict said as Asgeir retched and spewed in a trail as the Pict shoved him forward toward the vikings. One of Tormod's men unbuckled the brass clasp of the swordbelt, and they pulled the leather straps from him.

"This is the sword of the Gael-Slayer," Asgeir said. Tormod wrung his mouth.

"Helvete – I said I don't need that. Lothlend's huskarl will come for us if we take it. I'll take something else," Tormod said and looked wolfishly at the mead-hall.

Earp kept a hairy bare foot on Asgeir's back.

"Good work – what's your name?" Tormod asked the Pict.

"Earp."

"My thanks, Earp," Tormod said, "I'll be taking you – and freeing you, if you work for us."

"Aye," Earp said as he shoved his foot down harder on Asgeir's back and pressed him into the mud.

Asgeir found Eirik several paces afield, downcast, mouth open and muttering to himself.

"What should be done?" Earp asked.

"He's been punished enough, Earp. He's earned his bruises. No doubt he will run to his father, tail twixt the legs and mewling, but if we let him alone now, there will be no blood feud."

"So be it," Earp said.

"Victorious men!" Tormod cried. "We eat good tonight!"

The quiet bay erupted into a clamor. Men stomped up and down the fields and herded two cows down from the hills. Tormod, sword drawn, ripped open the door to the hall to a chorus of shrieks as he vanished into the haze of hearthfire smoke, and the hoary-faced man followed him in. Out marched a line of thralls, Toke's Pictish women and girls.

Earp kept his beefy hands on Asgeir's shoulders, the stench of the thrall rose over the blood and glop. Nine men guarded the defeated at spearpoint.

An elderly she-thrall stitched up the stubbed arm of the handless man. One of Tormod's men, no older than fourteen winters, stole over with the severed hand in his bloody sleeve and slapped it around a bit. All of the men laughed, even Earp, who laughed the hardest.

"You betray us so easily, Earp?" Eirik asked, his eyes downcast.

"I have want to betray a master at the promise of freedom, and this newcomer pissed me off."

"Enjoy your freedom, but Toke shall avenge us, Earp," Eirik said.

"Unlikely," said a viking with a blond mustache. "They say the Jarl's been lost to sea. Or else why would he be gone for so long? We leave you alive for goodwill. We have what we need."

"My father will hear about this," Asgeir said, "and he will carve the eagle on all of your backs."

The vikings said nothing. They looked about. One turned to the ship, while Earp worked to pluck off the barnacles from its hull.

"That's right, cower at it," Eirik said and now he eyed them. "Harald will put an end to all of this. No more raids. No more thievery. No more vikings."

"Maybe," the same viking said, "but we're hungry."

Some men carried a crate over to the ship, others with sacks of cereals. The wide door of the hall opened, and a line of sheep trotted out, followed by Tormod. The captain had a sword in one hand and a limp white chicken by the neck. From the eastern entrance of the hall, near the kitchen, the hoary-face man herded out a row of dark-haired women.

"Halt, ladies!" Tormod said and clasped the arm of Drusticca. "I'll take this one for myself – I am the victor, after all!"

The girl looked back with big blue watering eyes. The wind blew her plaits askew over her face.

"No," Eirik said with a cracked voice, "I beg for your mercy, Tormod. Not her."

"Why not?"

"She's my sister."

"A shame. I feel merciful today, but I like the looks of her."

Eirik writhed until he found his footing, stood up, and fell upon his knees at the muddy shoes of Tormod.

"Please."

"No."

"Please!"

Tormod placed the muck-encrusted sole of his shoe on the face of Eirik and nudged, and left a footprint on his forehead.

"I'm growing testy. The earth already drank blood today, maybe it needs some more?"

"You said you were hungry."

Tormod looked at the Pictish girl up and down. "I can't wait to taste her!"

His vikings laughed as Eirik sprang to his feet, but Tormod prodded the blade tip into his chest.

"Duel me then for her, as you did Asgeir."

Tormod said nothing. The lines of his face creased. "You've lost already, Eirik of Jarl Toke's farm. Blame yourself. Or your master. Or the son of Hallgeir."

Eirik pivoted and embraced his sister. She sobbed dryly onto his shoulder as he held her until two of the vikings pried him off.

"Drusticca," Asgeir said, "I swear by Thor that I will rescue you!" Eirik shouted.

"And by Ullr, I will get back my honor," Asgeir said. "The Gael-Kisser will come for you, Tormod."

Tormod's company hoisted the lich of their fallen comrade as they started seaward toward their ship.

The hoary-faced man hummed as another viking sang, and they all belted out:

Hungry sea-wolves are we,

Oars and blades make us free,

By our dead the meat sears,

When we hail lord of spears!

A train of men lifted the sheep up over the gunwale one by one, while Tormod stood astern along with Drusticca.

"Farewell, brother," she said. "Cease your worries – White Christ protects me."

By the gods – why did Earp betray Eirik? I could have stood in that doorway, watching like Heimdall, and died in her defense, rather than allow Eirik to live through this shame. I owed it to them, as their watchman, no matter how I ended up here. My poor friends, and that poor lass – this must not go unavenged.

Tormod's vikings kept their spears aimed at the survivors as they backed away knee-deep in the tide, then they clambered up the ship. The light-craft set sail from the beach as the rowers stroked from the bay, their song carried downwind back to the hillock where Asgeir, Eirik, and the other men just onlooked as the tide passed the ship across the sound.

CHAPTER V

The God of Plenty

The oil-lamp flickered and dappled Eirik's dark face as he sat slumped over at the table. Asgeir sipped at the sour ale, cloaked in heavy wool as he shivered. The chest he sat on had a loose lid, for it had been ripped open by a viking. The handless man knocked over a cup and ale rolled across the table and into his lap. He muttered. A girl sobbed in the kitchen corner of the mead-hall as the she-thralls busied about to cook the scraps of food overlooked by the raiders.

"Our last meat," Eirik said, "from a lamb that fell off a cliff and those fucking vikings missed it. But we have no sheep to breed now."

"And two heads of cattle gone," said one man.

"And nearly all of our harvest," said another.

"And stockfish," said another.

"And my fucking sister!"

Eirik's hit his head against the table edge, and his ale cup spilled over. Two women sobbed now from the kitchen.

"These rassragr! If they just asked us for food, we would have opened our cloaks for them, by Freyr, we would never let guests starve. Instead, they rob us and now we starve. I must thank Frigga that my mother and Fina are still with us. Drusticca," he said and leaned his head back and then slammed his fist again on the oak table. "And you know what's almost worst? What hatred chews at me, like worms on a corpse? That Earp betrayed me."

"We have to right this," Asgeir said.

"Where the fuck is Jarl Toke?" Eirik asked. "How could he leave the Orkneys for so long?"

"We can send a messenger to the South Islands, where my father is huskarl of Lothlend."

"In the winter? Who braves Cape Wrath early in the year? Let it alone, man."

"Let it alone?" Asgeir said as his knuckles reddened on the table's edge.

"Let it alone!" Eirik shouted as he slammed both his palms on the table. The oil of the soapstone lamp swelled over and ate the wick, and Eirik cradled his head in his arms on the unlit table.

Fina walked over with a brand and relit the fire.

Poor Fina, to see her sister dragged off by some viking. The blood rushed into his face, each vein pulsed in his nose. *Blast you to Helvete, Earp.*

"You lost that duel, Asgeir," Eirik said through his elbows. "What use are you?"

Asgeir lost his breath for an eyeblink and stuttered. "And if I won?"

"Doesn't matter, you lost, you loser."

Asgeir nearly grabbed hold of the table and shoved it over, but another spoke.

"We're all losers," he said.

For a spell, Asgeir sat and watched the roasting lamb. Fina turned it on its spit, the flames danced about and the firewood shifted underneath, sending it all aspark. That was all the food they had there.

"I'm overwintered here," Asgeir said. "Come fair weather, I leave, but I must help you and Drusticca, Eirik."

I arrived at this farm as a thrall, and by my bloodline, I walked as a free man and served as a watchman. I can forget past blemishes, for I can't bear to see my friends suffer. He stood up, drained his ale cup, and vaulted upon the chest. The loose lid ground along with his teeth.

"We outlived today – by Thor – I thought so, but you may as well be dead. Where was the fire within you when you met those vikings? What alights you now, after you felled one with a javelin? Which God do you worship, who accept you as so flabby and weak?

"What lawless men! They rode lawlessness like Odin rides the worlds. And your sister," Asgeir leaned over the table, the candlelight licked at his chin, "your sister is forced to ride him!"

Eirik rose from his seat as he snorted, while the men around the table gasped.

"Now you are alit, Eirik. What will you do about it?" Asgeir asked.

"There's nothing to do, but you ought not to be crass," Eirik said.

"Who are these men?" Asgeir asked.

"I don't know, I've never seen him or his ilk before. Their undyed sail and mismatched shields tell us nothing."

"We must find out who they are," Asgeir said as he pivoted and seized a spear from a rack of the wall. He jammed it, point-first, into the oak table, and all the men seated winced around it. "What of the Leidang? That out-sailed and overtook Ulf and his Sea-Bitch?"

"Audun, the huskarl, called it – I have no right to do so. We must wait for Jarl Toke."

"Enough with Jarl Toke! The man is missing – maybe lost! Our bellies will grow hungry, and our weapons will want for blood. We will find them, we will attack them, we will win, and your sister will be returned to your side."

"This newcomer talks much," the handless man said.

"Let him," Eirik said, and ran his fingers through his hair. "He fought fiercely, he deserves his say, just as any of you."

A silence hung over the hall as Asgeir, perched upon the chest, shivered at the knees. He shoved the spear forward, and it knocked into the unlit iron lamp that overhung the table. The lamp whirled about on its chain, and Asgeir waited until one of Eirik's men stood up.

"We've been wronged. How can we live with ourselves?"

Floki the Handless stood up as well. "Rassragr! I want revenge!"

Soon the other men all stood, save Eirik, and Asgeir found the shadows stilled from the hearth. Fina stood there, at the ready, hailing with a hot poker.

Eirik still sat. He glanced at Floki's bandaged stump.

"Yes, and with no hand, you will swing an axe, stroke an oar, and wipe your ass," he said with a laugh, and put his head back into his arms.

Asgeir rolled across the table, landed on his feet, and gripped Eirik by his shoulders.

"We leave whether you want us to or not."

Eirik closed his eyes and breathed heavy through his bulbous nose. He sniffled with all of the hairs of his nostrils adance.

"Raiding is lawlessness. Jarl Toke forbids us to raid each other. For good reason. We don't know where he is, so we can't ask him to right this wrong. There's nothing we can do."

"To Helvete with the jarl!" Asgeir yelled, his spit in white globs on Eirik's black hair.

"What sort of jarl just ups and leaves his jarldom? What sort of jarl allows his people to get raided by vikings, and he's nowhere to be found? Is he dead? He may as well be, for a ghost or afterwalker would serve these islands better."

"You cannot speak so poorly about Jarl Toke."

"I have."

Eirik's eyes slitted. A log on the fire slammed down, embers sprung through the air, ash and soot poured out, and the hearthfire went aspark.

"Fina, watch the fire!" Eirik said.

The Pictish girl yelped and with her poker, tended to it.

"An unruly fire, a sign," Asgeir said. *These islands will be scourged by fire.*

"The aloofness of my sister is not a sign," Eirik said. "Drusticca, two heads of cattle, all the sheep, all the corn. What booty for just one dead man. I can't just let Drusticca be besmirched, I just can't let us have nothing to eat. I agree. By Tyr, God of honor, I agree.

"You're the son of the huskarl of the king of Lothlend, surely you can field warriors," he went on. "Have you not cousins here? Friends? Bastard sons of your father?"

Asgeir scrunched up his face; he had nearly smote Eirik for that insult. *Father would leave no bastards!*

"No, but we must go after them, too few or not. We can make a plan. We can pray to Tyr for justice."

"And do what if we catch them? Us nine against seventeen again? It worked well, when our flank was overwhelmed."

"Tormod wishes for fame through battle. We must play on that."

"What do you mean?"

"We'll lure him into another fight, and this time, we will win, for we are roused by anger."

Eirik stood up, stepped back a pace, and unsheathed his sword.

"Then it's settled. Let us go and alert Audun at Kirkwall, perhaps he will call the leidang. Methinks those vikings won't return to a vulture-pecked corpse, but Fina, you and the thralls will go guest at our neighbor's farm. We'll take our knarr and hunt them down. We won't come back until my sister and the cattle and the sheep and everything else – plus more – is ours!"

"We won't be able to fit all of that in our knarr," the handless man said.

"We'll fit it all into a ship – theirs – after we lean them over the gunwale, shove spears up their ass and out their mouths, and dump them into the wildest strait of Orkney!"

The men all shouted, and Asgeir joined.

"Let me come too, Eirik," Fina said as she loped over, the hot poker in her hand swirling about like a sword.

"You jape? And the roast!"

Fina gasped and spun the lamb over on its back. The flametongues had charred its pink belly.

"But please, I want to go along with you!"

"What can you do?"

"Something! I can't just sit here while Drusticca is…"

"Are you daft?" Eirik asked and stole over to her, sheathing his sword. He took her by her bronze hand. "Don't you know what those vikings will do to you?"

"I'd stab them!" she said and thrust the hot poker. "Right in the balls!"

Eirik laughed, he laughed hard, but when the flames of the fireplace spilled into his eyes, Asgeir saw tears. Eirik turned from his men and wiped them away with his soft-hued yellow cuff.

"We need rowers and fighters."

"I can cook for ye, I can sew your clothes," she said, her Pictish twang soaked her words.

"It's too risky, I love you too much," Eirik said and let her hand go. He went back to the rest of them around the table.

"Agreed, Eirik. Nothing dreadful must happen to sweet Fina," Asgeir said.

"It's settled then. By Tyr, this injustice will not go unpunished. We will walk like the trickster, shunned by the gods he may be, and they will get what's coming to them."

They all sat down at the table as the she-thralls funneled out of the kitchen with wooden plates of buttered flatbread.

What has befallen Orkney, where roving bands of vikings raid? They said they were hungry and wanted food – their derelict ship, their ragged clothing, their drawn faces... were they telling the truth? My father always said hunger brings out the beast in men – they still stole the poor lass.

He recalled back on the doomed Sea-Bitch, when Ulf traded Éabhín, the Irish slave-girl for a pilot. Her white, thick calves trembled as she walked into the wee boat, never to be seen again. She swore she was no slave, but what rank had she been born into? Had she been a princess, her consort could send men Asgeir's way, but she disliked him, anyway, but he had saved her from a horrid death of drowning in the river back in Laerdal. Nevertheless, she was of no help as a slave.

The heftiness of the day and blow to the face hauled Asgeir into sleep. Ulf stood upon the cracking deck of the Sea-Bitch. His gaunt face frowned as he plummeted downward, seaward, into the depths below when the hull cracked in twain. The Sea-Bitch drank him that day, like a fly floating in a cup, unseen by its drinker. For an eyeblink, Asgeir found Ulf walking the seabed. His skin melted off his skull, his eyes naught but black gulfs, he afterwalked, his sparse gray hair floated about him like a crown. Afterwalker – the restless dead that haunt the living for they had never achieved their goal in life. *"I'll come for you, lad."*

"Asgeir!" Eirik shouted him awake.

"You've gotten walloped," a black-bearded man said and ran a finger over the swollenness of Asgeir's face. "Ol' Earp got you good. You must be dazing."

The firespit creaked as Fina turned the roasting the lamb just behind Asgeir. The aroma filled his nostrils with meat, and he savored it. Svartganger sped across the stone-linteled floor that ran adjacent to the longhearth. He jumped up on Asgeir's lap, fuzzy-coated from the rain. He sniffed about with his pink nose, and purred.

Such a good little mouser! I'll bring you, too, my friend. You're the luckiest cat I know, so we have another adventure ahead of us.

"The sea will make a man out of you yet, boy," Ulf had said.

Asgeir was still gripping the table edge, even as he petted the cat. How did he stand up to them and rallied them? Was Ulf right? *Calm seas don't make good sailors.*

The thralls dragged the faering from the turf-built boathouse at the choppy bay. Bestride the landing-place, the long Pictish graveyard lay, dotted by small cairns. Asgeir had learned the Picts buried their dead in the ground with little fare, nothing for their journey but the clothes on their backs, for they believed they would afterwalk when the world ended. His countrymen still buried their dead in the olden ways. The cairns and the mounds and the ship-shaped stones marked their own from the Picts.

"Why did you bury them there, in the Pictish graveyard?" Asgeir asked as he dragged the loose-lidded chest along the strand toward the boat. The men had been stocking the small boat with sea-clothing, and chests for them to sit on.

"The first Nordmann Jarl, Rolf the Older, who the island is named after, wanted to show the Picts who owns this land," Eirik said.

"I didn't realize you were even a Pict, until your sister told me."

Eirik shrugged. "I speak and think and dream Norse, I dress like a Nordmann, I pray to Thor to guide us on this journey. But I suppose I am still a Pict, since my parents were."

Asgeir wondered what his grave would look like, if they faced the vikings again and lost the fight. Perhaps then, he would not escape death. For a spell, he found himself in a grave, a shield behind his head like a pillow, Gael-Kisser in his clean hands.

A black-bearded man walked back, back-carrying a long rug, with a baby-faced man lugging along the other end. They both sweated and grumbled as they hoisted it into the faering.

"Eirik, why are we bringing this heavy thing?" Eirik's crewman asked.

"It's the only piece of riches those vikings left alone – it was woven in Miklagard – an heirloom from Jarl Toke's mother. We can gift it for allies, perhaps, if we can send messengers to Hjaltland, or Cat's Ness, or Sunderland."

Inside the boat, the men stuffed the hold with the rug along with foodstuffs and other supplies. Asgeir carried Svartganger by the scuff and set him down, sat upon the chest, and took up an oar with a cracked blade. The five other men all sat at the rowlocks, besides Floki the Handless, who would pilot them instead of rowing.

"A prayer to Njordr, provide us with safe passage, and we will provide you with sacrifice," Sigurd the Handless said.

Njordr – you came to me in that dream before we sank. Visit me again, and let me know my fate.

Their oars pierced the gray sea. Asgeir squinted in the sideways wind and rain that spat at them. They crossed the sound, toward a small island with a ruined monastery. A small boat was beached on its grassy shore, and as their seacraft rowed from the shelter of the ness of Rousay, a westward current burst against the boat.

Asgeir rowed with Eirik and his men throughout the afternoon. Their boat braved the choppiest waters of Orkney to the mainland, where they followed the coastline. Even the hardiest vikings wouldn't brave the west coast of Orkney in winter, in this windy weather, so they sailed due east, toward Kirkwall, where the old church lay in ruin in a bustling port. As they neared, they found a rope that ran west-east, barring all entry. Asgeir knew that jarls or even petty chiefs would oftentimes block their ports in times of strife, or to demand landing fees.

"Blocked off!" Eirik said behind them from the bow. "We must turn back, now it is hopeless."

"Nay," Asger said, "we must find either land here or brave the westside of the island! Maybe, anyway, those vikings have something to do with it."

The winds changed directions each eyeblink, and their boat spindrifted. Asgeir's spear wound burned as he rowed on their side to right the boat. The prow glanced off the rope, and they rowed astarboard.

Asgeir stood up, wobbled, pulled a stave from a chest, and after many strikes, set it alight with an iron firestarter and a flint-flake. He waved it as all of the men shouted and called to the port.

On the mainland, a hall stood upon a wide sandy mound, a bump in the otherwise flat land, next to the crumbling church. Several large ships and some smaller boats had been dragged upshore. The men from the boat shouted and clapped, and Asgeir waved a torch. A small, wiry sailor, Magnus, seized hold of the flare with his teeth, climbed up the thin mast like a fleeing marten, and waved the flare.

Even from that range, Asgeir could tell the man-in-charge who stormed out of the house looked grumpy. He boarded a boat with four men, and rowed out toward the other side of the rope.

"The way is closed, turn back," he yelled at them when he came within earshot.

"Audun, good tidings!" Eirik shouted. "Why can't we land at Kirkwall?"

Audun's boat drifted close to the rope. Asgeir knew him from back when he had been captured after the Sea-Bitch sank. *The Jarl's huskarl.* He wore a heavy wool cloak wrapped about him, but a silver brooch glimmered at his shoulder.

"Because I said so, Feidelm," Audun said. "The weather is shit, anyway."

"I'm called Eirik, you know that. But we have horrible news! We were just raided, they took my sister – there are vikings afoot! Is that the meaning of this rope?"

"The way is closed. You won't be going after them."

"I know we're fewer," Asgeir said, "but we're angrier. Let us through, Odin demands to wet the day with blood."

"Odin demands nothing!" Audun shouted. "This is my landing-place, my hall, my port, my church – you can row yourselves back to Rousay. Or brave the east or west and wreck if that is what Odin demands!"

"How could you?" Eirik asked. "Good Audun, my sister has been taken! You must call up the Leidang!"

"You don't understand," Audun said, "and you can't. I must refuse you, without Jarl Toke's orders."

"Let us port over – we won't overstay – we just need to reach the sheltered shores of the south."

"He's been raided already," Asgeir said. "And Audun is worried that he will piss himself if they return."

"Asgeir, this is Audun Gray-Hood, huskarl to Jarl Toke," Eirik said, wide-eyed.

Audun ruffled his thick gray mustache over his mouth. "Why does your Gaelic thrall speak so freely?"

"I'm no thrall, I am Asgeir, son of Hallgeir, huskarl to the King of Lothlend."

"Hallgeir has no power here, and neither does his son. You want passage, but deal insults."

"I wished for more passion from a jarl's huskarl," Asgeir said.

Audun pointed toward them, and his rowers reached the line in three strokes. The prow of their boat grazed the rope. The man had leathery skin, with a red scar that cleft his beard in twain under his left cheek. He threw the cloak back, and it flopped over in its sogginess, to reveal a weather-beaten scabbard with a sword, many dinks in its iron pommel.

"Men have been slain for less," he said.

"Attempt to slay me – if you dare," he said, and wondered why Odin had struck him so hard with spear-lust. *I lost against that Tormod, shield-bash or not, and this Audun is grizzled.*

Audun rested his beard upon his hand so that each long strand looked like hanging seaweed. The firelight from the flare still flickered as Magnus descended down the mast.

Audun stared Asgeir down. All quieted save for the rumble of the waves and the wind that whistled and juddered the rigging. "There's been enough blood today."

"Grant us passage then," Asgeir said. "Odin himself guises as a guest. Can you really turn us away?"

"We've had enough of you vikings," Audun said. "You are sadly right, I cannot turn away a guest. I'll grant you passage. Get on, then, and join us for a meal."

Audun's men rowed eastward to the headland, and one rower unhooked the rope that girded the bay. The taut rope went limp and vanished down the murky depths.

"He's a seasoned warrior," Eirik said.

"I could tell," Asgeir said.

"He would have killed you," Eirik said and spat into the sea.

"We press on, Eirik."

"You're right, Asgeir, whatever it takes to kill that bastard that took Drusticca."

Landward, one of Audun's men grabbed hold of the bow of the faering and helped drag it back to land.

Asgeir and the men warmed themselves on the benches around the crackling long-hearth. Above it, an iron cauldron, where Pictish thralls ladled soup into wooden bowls. Red-painted shields adorned the walls of the longhouse, and a walrus-skin rug splayed out on the floor. Audun himself sat at a high-seat with twin pillars, carved in the images of Freyr and Freya. He ate warm stew from a soapstone bowl, his food strewn about his gray mustache. Pictish thralls handed them soup in wooden bowls.

"That Tormod is more than a nuisance," Audun said and wrung the soup from his mustache. "He's a viking without a target. Like an udder without a bucket to milk it. I warned him not to raid Toke's farm, I, the huskarl of the Toke, and he disobeyed me, and betrayed the jarl."

"You had forewarning of this?" Asgeir said, his bowl nearly falling out of his hands.

"There was nothing I could do."

"My sister was taken, Audun," Eirik said. He hadn't eaten, and he shivered despite the warmth of the hall. "Who knows what they did with her."

"And we have naught to eat," Magnus said.

"Men will starve this winter, By Red Thor!" Audun smashed the soapstone bowl against the floor. The bowl cracked in half, and soup splashed into the fire and sizzled. "Tormod and his men were hungry, too."

"And so they can just take it, unlawfully, from someone else? So they can just spill blood?" Asgeir asked.

"There's nothing we can do. There's not a thing we can do in Hel's shady realm. The harvest was lacking this year – we should have offered more to the gods – but some of Toke's men turned Christian."

"Why would they do that?" Asgeir asked.

"A lot of them took Pict wives, and they're Christian. It's a lot easier – you know, strife in the house, strife on the land. Nevertheless, the crops failed, and the jarl is missing."

"This is no fault of ours," Asgeir said. "Why should we pay for it? Why should Drusticca?"

"The gods hate the unlucky," Audun said with a sneer as he kicked his birch-bark shoe off one foot.

"What of the Svears of Deerness?" Eirik asked. "With the queer hats? Those outlaws wouldn't back down from a scrap."

"I mistrust their leader," Audun said, "more so than Tormod. His tongue is quick, and it belies dishonesty."

"Surely," Asgeir said as he swallowed his stew, "Orkney has a Leidang, the levy of all free, weaponed men can be called by the assembly, just like in Norway. They can bring that viking under the law."

Audun just stared at the thin log in the fire.

"We swore to Tormod that we wouldn't call up the Leidang."

Asgeir gasped. "Just who is the huskarl here?"

All fell silent save for the fire. A log split and sparks strewn about the stone-paved floor. Asgeir saw the shield behind the seat of Audun on the wall. The iron boss had been bashed in, and much fray around the rawhide edge spoke of battles.

"Asgeir," Eirik said in an undertone, "he'll have you killed."

Audun stared at Asgeir, one eye twitching. For a moment, Asgeir had seen the Grim One about him, the one-eyed God Odin, whose mood changes like the wind. Just like the Jarl Haakon. Yet that jarl was no coward, and Odin hated cowardice.

"That's the second time you've insulted me – and now as a guest in my home."

Asgeir balked at that. "Forgive me for that, Audun, but why did you let them get the best of you?"

"You don't understand, by Thor!" he shouted as he slammed his fist onto the pillar of Freyr. It wobbled, but stood steadfast. "You don't understand," he said to Asgeir.

"Then allow us understanding," Eirik said, "else we will leave here thinking the worst of you."

"Have you not heard the news from Norway? The King at Karmøy, Harald Finehair, declared that no scissors shall snip his hair until all of Norway is united. There have been too many quarrels, which turn to raids, which turn to battles, which turn to wars. There shall be no more unruly jarls, no more squabbling cocks over hens, no more wars.

"Think about what it means for Orkney – Denmark has had a king for over a hundred years. The Saxons didn't – when was the last time you heard of the Saxons? Charlemagne clipped their bulls into oxen. And the Wends don't fare better. Then look at Angeland – petty kingdoms – sticks without a strap to bundle them into a faggot – and then along came the Danes, Nordmenn, Welshmen, Skotts. And too, your grandfathers, the Pictish chiefs, Feidelm, were not united, and were no match for mine."

Eirik sat hunched over, his eyes ablaze.

"If Harald unites Norway – do you know what he will do? What will happen to all jarls who shirk from at his crown? He'll hammer them like Charlemagne on the Saxons.

"Yes," Audun said as he stretched back. "And he'll come for us next. Word has it that he considers the Orkneys a spoke of his wheel."

If he considers Orkney, then he must consider Hjaltland, and the South Isles, my home! What will become of my father? Papa wouldn't submit to a king.

"The reason my family ventured here when I was young was because we disliked how our jarl in Troendelag ruled. He taxed too much and he had his nose in our business. No one really bothered us here. Sure, the Picts needed to be whipped," Audun said with a motion of his hand. Eirik raised his lip at that. "And we had quelled the monks since they never stop blabbing about the White Christ, and we had to grab the headlands to defend and ward off against the Skotts. But we were left alone."

"You reckon everyone will just keep it quiet? Of course he'll hear of this," Eirik said.

"We already called up the leidang to ward against vikings just recently. If this raid becomes a battle, and that becomes a war, then surely he will," Audun said. "He has many friends, his allies grow in numbers, his links forged like chains. He is king of the southwest, where all stuffs flow in and out of the Nordvegr. Logs to his fire."

"We're going after Tormod, and you can't stop us," Asgeir said as he drained the last of his soup. "I thank you for your hospitality, and I am sorry for the earlier insult. But I am son of the huskarl of Lothlend, and I will have my honor."

"It's foolhardy," Audun said. "Why don't you sit back down, and let me tell you something?"

Asgeir balked. *What's he mean? Something about my father?*

"You're Hallgeir's boy. I got that. I knew your father. Not very well, but in my first few seasons in what was once Pictland, I got to know him. He is a fine warrior, and you're cut from the same cloth – the Red Thor is about you. Quick to anger, quick to fight, quick to passions. I was once like that, too."

"Kind words of my father are appreciated, Audun. I miss him, and I only hope that he may look upon me as an honorable warrior like himself."

"War has hardened him, Asgeir, and it will harden you, too. But peace has softened my heart. Now I am content to live the rest of my days free, happy, and home. I do my duty to ensure my family prospers. My wife died this winter – and I am afraid I am not too far after."

"With a heavy heart, I speak for us all when I say I am sorry," Eirik said. "But there is hope for Drusticca, Audun, even if you don't live much longer. We must go after Tormod."

Audun sighed. "He came here brazen, like a stallion who trampled his rival and mounted his mare. Some of the lads here joined him, and they went off to raid Birsay."

"What? How could they dare?" Eirik asked. "Birsay is perched on a cliff-surrounded island and the only way to the island is during low tide, and even then, they must cross the strand."

"The jarl is missing," Audun replied. "Tormod smelled weakness, and the sea-wolves seek its scent."

"We follow them, then – and strike them when they try to pass the foreshore," Asgeir said. "Tell me, Audun, could you deny this from your guests? Could you turn us away, when we need you so much?"

Audun slumped down in his chair, strummed his hand, then bolted back up.

"Asgeir, your words ring true. I'm off with you then – men – arm yourselves – since no man should walk unarmed in this whirling world. Maybe I'll get them to stand down for you, and we evade bloodshed."

"Then we set off," Asgeir said. *Audun thinks many steps ahead, and I feel he sees Harald as king already.*

"We must be hasty," Eirik said and rose up. "Come, Audun Seven-Fingers. Let us put an end to this viking business, and right these wrongs that are happening in our lawless land."

Audun sat grim-faced for a spell, strummed the rest of his chair, and stood up. "Perhaps Harald should," he said, but stopped himself from speaking more.

"Come on, then, son of the Gael-Slayer, and Feidelm, now Eirik, of Jarl Toke," he said to the two men. "Gather up your lads. We have enough crew for a faering, so we follow your boat."

The log split in twain on the fire and embers flared about.

"Then it settles it, Eirik," Asgeir said to him. "I'll get my honor back by defeating Tormod, return Drusticca to you, then set forth to find my father myself."

"And I'll be at your side along the way," Eirik said, "for I cannot repay you enough for helping me and Drusticca."

The Picts rolled the two boats across the trackway, upon logs. After the stern of each boat had reached one log, another replaced it, until the boats rumbled. They pushed uphill to crest the mainland, and then back downhill, until they rolled to the other side. They hit the sandy beach where the mounds lay, and as Asgeir trudged through the sand, his feet nearly ankle-deep in some places, they passed a crooked mound a ship's length away. The rain had lightened, though the wind blew a screen of sand off the mound.

Something white flickered among the yellow-brown sand. Asgeir focused on it through the sand drifts. Bleached bones. The top half of a round, broken man's skull, and below, a yellowed yawning grin.

"Why is there a skull just sticking out of the mound?" Asgeir asked.

Eirik bit his lip. "It's our alderelder. The sidhe send the winds to ruin their graves whenever they believe they've been wronged. To warn us that death is ever near."

"It must be Tormod," Asgeir stated.

"No, something else comes… I can feel it," Eirik said as he heaved while the boat ground over the sand into the water.

They scurried over the hull, seized their oars, and rowed.

"You can feel something evil?" Asgeir asked. "But you're a man, no volva."

"You Nordmenn believe that to be a woman's power, but the Picts think a man can do it, too."

Audun shifted the rudder, and sat down to row as the wind caught their single sail and set the course toward Ophir. They rowed up the canal that veered westward. They slowed to the scrubland there, where a patchwork of farms lay spread throughout the land upon green mounds. The shoreline broke at a hook, with a span of yellow sand where the furious ocean calmed on both sides, like the resting hands of a maiden. Beyond the strand, a ship with a furled sail lay beached. Tormod the Colorless's ship.

A whirlwind of puffins blackened the sky over the rocky, cliffy islet. They darted about and skimmed over the choppy gray sea. Mist shrouded the horizon like unspun wool, and the wind bit as remorseless as a fox on shrew. Asgeir rowed hard, each stroke of the oar seemed to stretch the stitches in his wound. Audun's long gray beard fluttered in the breeze, over two layers of piebald, torn tunics, axe hung at his waist.

When the men rowed halfway to the end of land, Birsay emerged from the mist. A green lump fronted by beach and flanked by sea, and longhouses capped the islet. Stretched over the rocky cliffside, a staircase bowed and switch backed.

They rowed westward and bestride the island, and when they rounded the corner of land, they hugged the coastline northward. Even over the wind and calm sea, a horn mooed downwind from the puffin-donned island. Enemies sighted them.

"We must moot – amidships!" Audun walked over to the mast with Eirik nearby. Asgeir, eager to show them that Gael-Kisser deserved to be strapped to his waist, rose from his seat and met them there.

"It would be self-murder if we attack them. It is not called the fort island for nothing," Audun said, "they will not allow us to scale those rickety stairs. We must form a plan."

"We can play to Tormod's honor – demand that they meet us in pitched battle on the strand," Asgeir said. "Or let me duel him again."

"Nay," Eirik said, "you lost to him before, Asgeir."

"Listen, I am the huskarl to Jarl Toke," Audun said as he wrapped his arms around both the men. "Let us show up as guests, and then we cannot be turned away."

"He'll know us," Eirik said, "we just warred against him."

"And he won," Audun said, "and you have arrived to make amends."

Asgeir and Eirik looked at one another.

"I don't like this," Asgeir said, "may as well creep up behind him with a dagger in hand. We cannot just lie our way to victory!"

"And what do you say? We shall all die attempting to climb Birsay? And we do not know his numbers now."

"Then what? We murder him while he is aloof, like a coward?" Asgeir asked as the rain now pitter-pattered down upon them. Some of the sailors furled up the sail as the wind died.

"He may not be unreasonable. They wanted food – not to fight, let us speak to them," Audun said.

"You've misled us, Audun. You've taken us here to parley, not to fight," Asgeir said, "step aside, you old fool."

Audun failed to budge. Asgeir waited for his eyes to downcast and his heart to tremble, but his gaze stayed as still as the dead wind.

Asgeir unsheathed Gael-Kisser, but his foe just stood there.

"You wouldn't slay the huskarl of a Jarl," Audun said.

"Nay," Asgeir said, "I fight, not murder, and I fight men, and you are no man, but a coward."

Asgeir turned to Eirik, who bit his lip.

"What do you plan, Asgeir?"

"To redden Odin's spear," Asgeir said as he walked astern. They slunk away from the strand that linked the land to the islet. It drained out in streams and shallows as the ship ran aground nearby the grassy, mound-strewn shoreline.

"Sailors! Fetch rope and disembark! The day is young," Asgeir said as he realized he quoted Ulf, "and wanting of blood!"

Audun stood agog as the sailors flipped open the lids of chests and out came the rope. The sailors clambered down both sides of the ship after Asgeir.

The mushy sand sucked at Asgeir's shoes as he trudged on, beelined toward Tormod the Colorless's ship nestled in a naust. At the brim of the islet, a throng of men formed, spears aloft and shields at breast as if molded from clay.

"Attach the ropes, "Asgeir said, "and drag their ship away, that will draw them down here! Be hasty!"

The men looped the rope around the chipped, unadorned prow of Tormod's ship.

"Drag it – seaward!"

The sailors split into two teams of six and nine, with Asgeir leading the left-most. They pulled on the ropes in a grand heave, feet sloshed through shallow seawater as the hull of the ship edged toward the draining sea, its keel furrowing the sand in its wake.

A figure emerged from the promontory, swept down from the throngs of men, and strode wraithlike.

"Madness! Thieves! Stop!" Tormod shouted downwind.

"Don't listen," Asgeir said, "drag on, sailors! Let him squirm."

Movement scurried and hurtled down the stairs, a wave of men, armed as they reached the wet sand down between the lands. A horn blew, and Asgeir peered around the hull of the ship to find Tormod there, his stringy blond hair cast askew over his red face, a horn to his lips, blowing into it with lungfulls as if to bestow a spell upon them to cease. "By Tyr, we will have an honorable fight then, Tormod."

The sailors waded through the seawater now, and Asgeir halted them with a raise of his palm.

"Tormod! Come down and fight us," Asgeir shouted as they continued to drag the ship. "Or she gets set adrift!"

Tormod and a dozen of his men had funneled down the stairs halfway. They clustered behind their lord who walked several spans apace from them, and when he came within earshot of Asgeir, he drew the sword from his waist.

"Unhand my ship, you bastard!"

"Climb down and fight," Asgeir said. "The day is young and wanting of blood," he quoted Ulf again.

"Is it a battle you wish for?" Tormod said as he recognized Asgeir and Eirik. "One man fattened the worms today, and we sent him there. I, Tormod the Colorless, will feed the crabs and shrimp and seagulls."

"Poke your head out of your shell," Asgeir said, "the battle awaits here on the strand. We fight in honor of the God of Spears!" He turned to the men and raised his sword.

"And we have your oath that you will not fire arrows or throw javelins when we descend?" Tormod said.

"I would not forsworn that," Asgeir said. "No darts at all – let us settle this like men."

"So be it," Tormod said as he unsheathed his axe.

Asgeir and his men stood just twenty-seven men, most spear-armed and shielded. Asgeir paced to and fro along the shaping shieldwall, but Audun stepped forward.

"You rallied the men, son of Hallgeir, but I will command us."

"Nonsense," Asgeir said, "it was I who roused Eirik and his men, it was I who lured Tormod out of his nest."

"These are my men – and my people, you Norse-speaking Gael," Audun said with a glare. "Stand down."

I suppose he's right. He is more experienced. If that is what the Norns have decreed, then I will bide my time, until I can live up to the name of my father. Now, battle comes – pay attention! "Go on then, Audun, lead us to victory."

The mist thickened around the strand and enclosed it like two hands clapping. The armsmen of Tormod stepped down to the sand from the wooden stairs, one by one, until their battleline had stretched nearly thrice as long as Asgeir's own. They came in tens and Asgeir counted nearly forty, as he found himself abreast with Eirik and another man on the left flank of the line.

Upon this battlefield on the foreshore, between the cliffy islet and the steep hillside, little room remained for formations and ploys of the open field. The two sides would meet in that cramped space, a wall of spears and shields, with Odin alone who would decide the victor.

"Outnumbered, and the last time we lost," Eirik said.

"Shut up, man," Asgeir said, "have heart. The gods love the brave. Fina told me you wanted Valhal. This is that road."

"To the right flank, Asgeir!" Audun shouted, before Eirik could respond.

He wove out of the line. The right flank, where the eager, young, battle-frenzied men pushed and edged and neared to break through.

Asgeir found himself as the last man of the flank, as the lines stretched and nothing lay to his right but a rocky slope. He raised his shield until his eyes peered over its rawhide edge. He hadn't known the men that stood just out of spear's length before him. They appeared older, a grizzled man with a whitened neck rested a dry-shafted spear over his heavy leathered shield. Tormod had more men, both older and younger.

The sun glinted from behind the clouds and the bronze clamps over Asgeir's shield gleamed. The shadow of both ships cast in front of him as the two lines hemmed in one another. Tormod ran the ranks behind his enemy line, raising high with his knees. He waved a colorless banner hung from a dry-shafted spear, undyed wool, as if to mock Eirik's earlier words.

No javelins. No arrows. No slings. Spear to spear, iron upon iron, man against man.

The battlelines closed in toward each other while the briny breeze blew hard. Asgeir found the sand slick and slippery when he tip-toed through the wetness of it. The elder man sidestepped further rightward as they closed in on one another. He wore a brown patchy tunic, his gnarled hand loose around a spear. When they locked eyes, the old man sidestepped further and struck at Asgeir's flank, but he raised his shield and the point glanced off the leathered face. Asgeir winced as the wound trembled in his breast, the sting of it clouding and overburdening.

"Enemies! It's started!" someone shouted from down the line.

"Don't let him outflank you," a young man, no older than fifteen winters, said to Asgeir.

The old man had sidestepped again and readied for another strike.

Asgeir fanned out until he found himself against the scratchy ledge of the slope down to the strand. The wet sand sucked at his feet as he pivoted away from a strike from the old man. He knocked the shaft of the polearm down with his sword, leaving a gash in the wood, but his foe had reach on him.

All down the line, spears vied against shields. They cracked and banged and soon a rhythm of iron upon wood clanged out, sprinkled with grunts and groans and screams. All the while Tormod marched behind his backline, yelling orders, his colorless banner even less colorful in the growing mist. Audun, his axe on his shoulder, shouted downwind to his men with the stifled bays of a large dog.

Asgeir stepped to the right until he bumped against the rocky outcrop and scratched his wrist. He readied when a spear came for him, not from the old man, but a young one, thirteen winters. The spear struck his thigh. With a step backward, he found himself bunched up against the rockwall with his shield and sword all twisted. The spear bounced off his shield, and the old man's spear vied toward his head. Asgeir groaned in pain from the old spear wound as he poised his spear, and jumped back out of the line and pivoted from the wall to give himself space when the old man stepped forward.

"Hold him there!" he shouted to the young boy.

The boy dropped his shield and with both his hands swung the shaft of the spear like an axe and hit Asgeir's shield. Asgeir pushed forward but the shaft caught him off-balance and the old man's spear struck. Asgeir raised his shield but failed when his spear wound pain snapped. *Helvete! I can't lift my shield!*

He parried the next spear-blow with his sword. The boy pulled back the spear and stabbed at him. Asgeir thumped it away with the rim of his shield and backed into the line, as Audun yelled.

"Careful!"

Asgeir eyed the boy, who stared at him with a fiery gaze in his squinted blue pupils. Shieldless though with a revving spear, the boy waited to strike Asgeir, but a spear struck him in the side and he yelped and crumpled into a heap crying "Help!".

The old man turned to look at the boy. Asgeir raced forward now, and before his enemy could raise his shield to block or spearshaft to parry, Asgeir slashed him across his shins. The old man stumbled out of the line as Tormod shouted for some men to rush the flank.

"Careful – back, back!" Audun yelled.

Asgeir withdrew from the line, in haste, as two axe-armed men rushed forward at him. He knew they must back off to reform, to push on either flank.

Tormod withdrew his own men to halt the charge, and the lines crystallized again into two shieldwalls, a din of iron and wood and groans, with an undercurrent of feet shifting about the wet sand. The old man crawled away from the battle, streamlets of blood trickling through the sand.

The spearmen to Asgeir's left struck toward their enemies as the two lines vied spear against spear, the one-handed armsmen waiting to close the range and strike. Beads of sweat ran into Asgeir's eyes as one axeman looked beyond him. Not at him, not to his comrade spearman that stabbed and jabbed and parried, but as if in a trance. A gale knocked his square yellow hat off to reveal a tuft of blond hair, curly like kindle.

"Charge!" someone shouted as the blond axeman closed distance with Asgeir.

The spearman struck his weapon at the charging man, but he swung his shield and held the spearshaft down. Behind them, Tormod dropped his banner and unsheathed his axe.

"Charge!"

Three men rushed forward shield-first. They kicked up sand as they pummeled against the line with the force of a cow wallowing over a fence.

Their line bowed under Tormod's attack, and they found nowhere to retreat and reform but oceanward. The spearman next to Asgeir threw his weapon to the ground to surrender, and his enemies moved past him toward Asgeir. Tormod himself eyed him.

"Surrender!" Tormod shouted at Asgeir, and now several of his comrades retreated back, under the prow of Eirik's boat. "Surrender and you will live!" Tormod shouted.

Asgeir bumped into something soft and sweaty, and found Audun behind him. The old housecarl cast down his axe and shield. He shoved past Asgeir with his palms bared.

"Mercy!" he shouted with a rasp. "We are outnumbered – you have us!"

"No!" Asgeir shouted. *I must get my honor back. We must not lose another fight!* "Men," he yelled as Audun shouted something unheard, "surrender if you are a coward – fight on if you are Odin's own!"

Audun's men fought on. The line reformed and Asgeir found himself twixt two spearmen. Their line had thickened at the right flank but had been hook-shaped, with the left and center steadied, while the right bent like a crooked, cracked stick.

"Idiots," Audun shouted. He had fallen behind the enemy line, and knelt, weaponless. "You'll die here on the foreshore."

If I do, I die with honor.

Spears sang for Asgeir, in a melody of iron and a rhythm of wood, as they assailed his shield. His hand gripped the iron boss tight, his shield a step away from him, spearpoints striking all about like quills. Asgeir found his heels digging furrows in the wet sand as the enemy pushed them. Now the center of his line sank and Asgeir shot a glance at Eirik – an axeman whacked away at his shield and splintered chunks of wood, rawhide and leather, but the Norse-Pict stabbed underhand, below his shield's rim, and drove his spear into the knee of his foe. *He wants Valhal, then so do I.*

"We'll draw quarter," Tormod said, his axehead poking from under his shield.

"Hold them – push them back!" Asgeir said.

In a flurry, three men dropped their spears, drew their axes, and charged. Asgeir joined them. Gael-Kisser's blade hissed in the salty breeze and their iron swung for their foes. Tormod took one step backward, and Asgeir rushed him. In three bounds Asgeir had the rim of his shield against the face of Tormod's and pinned his sword arm behind. He poised Gael-Kisser to strike as spearpoints from Tormod's men rapped against his shield. His own axemen arrived at his flanks and they too struck. One axeman bashed a spearman's hands and then chopped his thigh and he crashed to the sand with a gurgle.

Asgeir struck at Tormod and when the viking chief parried he found his hand wound under his arm and his shield with it. Asgeir had caught him in a bind, the flat of Gael-Kisser under his arm, as useless as if he had been weaponless. But Tormod leapt backward and the two axemen harried against Asgeir. Their axeheads chopped at him. One axe split through the rawhide and stuck itself in the splintered beechwood as Asgeir's spear wound flared.

"Back!" Asgeir shouted through the pain, and the men withdrew. *The men listen to me, my father would be proud.*

The battleline had bowed again, the shieldwall thinner but tighter. The enemy hemmed in as Tormod repeated, "We will draw quarter! We will draw quarter!"

Just as Asgeir found the receding tide wrapped around his ankles, cold, Tormod ceased his plea. His enemies backed away, even as more of Asgeir's comrades threw down their weapons on the foreshore.

"Jarl Toke's men!" someone of the enemies cried.

The slosh of men-at-arms from behind Asgeir's battleline sounded. In the shallows of low tide, dozens of armed men waded in the water from a fleet of ships ran aground. The vanguard wore bright yellow riding-coats, swords in brass-fitted belts that sheened in the sunlight. A woman in a red-white dress soaked up to her waist held a banner, unseen to Asgeir for the wind had stilled.

"Retreat!" Tormod shouted. "Retreat! Too many of them! To the fort!"

"Don't let them," Asgeir said loud, "pursue them!"

"Kill them – kill Tormod! Where is Drusticca?!" Eirik shouted from afar as he raced headlong toward them.

The clamor of iron quieted as Tormod's men ran hard down the foreshore. Asgeir and his men chased after them, leaping over the broken spearshafts and dead and wounded men strewn over the beach like reddened shells. They veered toward the stairs up to Birsay. Asgeir placed himself twixt the enemy and the fort, sword aloft. Tormod and his men pivoted away, and ran for their ships in the boathouses at the far end of the foreshore.

I must cut them off – they cannot escape – Tormod, I won't lose to you again!

All alone, Asgeir outpaced him, running like a hound after a hare, and he put himself between the boathouses and Tormod's men. His men hurried after him, Eirik foremost, and there he met Tormod.

"Out of our way or I'll run you down," Tormod said as he brandished his axe.

"I have come to challenge you," Asgeir said. "Run me down if you dare – but I challenge your honor. Agree to duel me again!"

Tormod's face glowed red as if wind whipped. "If you move, so we may retreat, you will have your duel later."

Asgeir sidestepped away from the boathouses. Tormod let his axe slide back under his belt as he and his men seized the boats and dragged them to the other side of the foreshore. By the time Asgeir's reinforcements reached solid ground, Tormod the Colorless and his men had escaped in a faering and vanished into the gloomy mist of the sea.

"We win!" someone cried, and all the men shouted, their spears aimed skyward as they cheered.

A few had bested many, and Asgeir found himself brimmed in bloody pride on the gore-soaked strand. Yet his chance to vie against Tormod remained lost, and he hadn't found Drusticca.

"Rudolf High-Hat!" Audun cried as he rose to his feet at the arriving warriors. A yellow banner fluttered over them as they trudged through the blood-caked sand. *Not Jarl Toke – but Rudolf High-Hat? Arild's father? Frida's husband?*

A storm of men roved across the foreshore and herded a handful of stragglers from Tormod's vikings. Three of them. One with a broken spearshaft through his forearm. Another shoeless and bleeding from his feet. The dark third had clots strewn about his bright beard.

The men parted in twain for Rudolf High-Hat. He walked the avenue of men, his woad-blue, stiff pointed hat a head high off his skull, capped in a silver cone. He was sworded at the waist, slender of shoulder, lithe like a cat, wrapped in a long red coat, and a fresh cut scarred his hatchet-like, short-bearded face.

Asgeir stood midway across the sward with the heaving, sweating men.

"You let him go," Rudolf said with a stiffened glare at Asgeir.

"I had to," Asgeir said, "by Ullr, God of duels."

Rudolf turned and spat. He readied a spear toward the three captives now centered among the victors.

Someone elbowed through Asgeir and Eirik. Audun, heaving, his white beard beaded in blood. "Rudolf, sheath your sword! I, Audun Seven-Fingers, housecarl of Joke Toke, forbid more killings!"

The Svear lord cast a glance at Audun and turned back to the captives.

"You," he said to the first man. "Three words on why you should live."

"I am wounded," he said.

"Not enough. You die for Odin."

Rudolf stabbed him through the chest with his spear. Gasps rippled through the crowd, both victors and defeated. Audun took a step forward, but a youth grappled him from behind, and ushered him away from the killing ground.

The wounded man mouthed soundlessly. Two of Rudolf's men, clean and bloodless, dragged him away further down the shore.

Rudolf nodded to the next man.

"I find no words," the captive said.

"For Odin," Rudolf said.

His spear cracked against the ribs of the man in a *thunk*. Rudolf drew it back and jabbed him again. The man fell to the ground in shivering death throes.

Before Rudolf could speak, the third man laughed.

"I have words," he said, "and more than three. For Odin I go, then I die with a jest across my lips – the man who has a tall hat has a short cock."

Rudolf's men gasped, and some shouted blackened words. They all crowded around the lone enemy, who stood athwart them, weaponless but mirthful.

Asgeir laughed as he drew closer. *The voice of that captive – he sounds so familiar!*

The man spread his arms. Rudolf lowered his spear, cast it aside, and drew his sword. The defeated man failed to wince. He was blond and broad, standing a head taller, two men wider, and had a yellow round-clipped beard. Hatless, his wavy hair danced in the wind. He half-grinned down at Rudolf.

"If you do not fear death, then I ought to chop your cock off, and you'll be as boneless as King Ivar," Rudolf said. "And a boar tusk twixt your legs for the rest of Midgard's days. What say you?"

"I say you'd not find a boar tusk big enough to fit over my balls," he said with a laugh. "Go on, scrawny, chop me down, if that twig arm of yours is strong enough!"

I know him. I've met him before. He looks so familiar. He sounds like someone I've known! But who is he?

Rudolf grimaced.

"Go on – send to me Valhal!"

"Odin will not have you among our heroes. You're unworthy. You have made too much evil mischief."

"I was simply a guest defending my host at Birsay! I speak with honesty – for a man to be sent to Odin shall speak no falsehoods! It was his mistress that egged Tormod on like a rider and pizzle."

"And who is this mistress?" Rudolf asked him.

"My tongue cannot betray my host, good Rudolf," he said. "I told you enough of the truth, but let me not die a traitor."

"You will not die," Rudolf said and sheathed his sword. "I believe you. And a good guest you were. Now I will pardon you if you fight alongside me. Will I forgive your insults? Hardly, but one does not have to like his warriors. Tell me, then, is this mistress at Birsay?"

"Why, I cannot betray her hiding place," he man said, "though I am grateful that you spared me, despite my insults."

"We shall feast tonight," Rudolf said and to that the big man laughed.

"By Freyr – good! I am not disloyal, but I hold no loyalty to Sigurd, merely was I a guest to the mistress of Birsay." The man took a bow.

Rudolf cast a glance over his men. "Go on then – before the tide turns and we all get our feet wet." He turned a glance to Asgeir and Audun. "And newcomers, we have much to discuss."

"Rudolf High-Hat," Audun said, still heaving, war-shock splattered across his face. "We are thankful you arrived. We were almost killed! We wished to surrender, but…"

"But what?" Rudolf asked.

"This lad here, he refused us to surrender, even though it was hopeless."

Rudolf looked from Asgeir to Audun, then back to Asgeir.

"Why did you do that?"

"For honor," Asgeir said.

"They said they'd draw quarter," Audun said.

"Did we know he was telling the truth? As my father said, only swords speak true," Asgeir said. The former enemy captive looked at him sidelong.

"We thought Jarl Toke had come to our rescue," Audun said. "We didn't know Rudolf High-Hat was arriving."

"But I did arrive," Rudolf said. "The Gods love the bold. Good on you – never surrender," he said to Asgeir. "Let your wrathfulness strike the enemy even after death."

"I am Asgeir, son of Hallgeir the Gael-Slayer."

"And I am Hallgeir!" the former captive shouted.

In one bound, Hallgeir hauled him into the air. Trunk-like arms squeezed around him, the globs of blood smeared over Asgeir's face as his father nuzzled him cat-like. Gael-Kisser slipped from his hand.

"Pappa?"

"It is me, Asgeir!"

"Pappa," Asgeir said as his eyes welled, but he blinked that away when he found the hardened men around them agaze in curiosity. "I prayed to Thor hard that I'd see you again!"

"He saw you through then!" Hallgeir hugged him tight and pulled back. "Come on, son, you will celebrate your victory tonight!"

"They nearly killed you!"

"Nearly is never good enough!" Hallgeir said with a laugh.

"But why were you fighting for that viking?"

Hallgeir laughed even harder. "Simple loyalty to my host – but let's leave. As Rudolf said, we'll be swimming if we wait here. Come on."

It's so hard to say something, when there is so much to say, Asgeir thought as he followed his father up the steps. To his surprise, Hallgeir wore naught but a thin linen tunic that hung down past his knees and no leggings or shoes. He had a red silk headband around his head, and a necklace with a single jet bead.

They walked across the bloodied, furrowed sand as the water spilled across the strand. Asgeir climbed the wooden stairs, rendered rickety by the weight of the warriors thrown about it when they ran down to meet them. The trail switchbacked until they arrived upon a greensward of the tidal islet.

Before Asgeir could gather the courage to ask his father a thing, a rapping overwhelmed Birsay.

The womenfolk and children had gathered around a simple stone building with a skewed entrance. Beyond, a cluster of longhouses surrounded a hall, and beyond that were the cliffy swards where a sheep herd grazed.

"Out of my way – all of you," Rudolf said to two women. He drew his sword in a hiss, and they shirked away.

He lunged over to the door of the square, stone-built building. A thin cross had been carved across it. He knocked hard with the brass pommel of his sword.

"Come out at once, you stirrer of storms."

A muffled voice called back at him.

Rudolf tapped the cross with his pommel. "That sign scares me not. My god is not yours – I'll set the roof of this Christian hof alight."

He pounded hard on the wooden door that rumbled on its hinges until it opened, and a shadowed woman skittered from the next pommel blow.

"Unarm yourself!" a voice shrieked from within the dark building.

"Unarm your tongue," Rudolf said. "I have had a gore-filled day, and enough of your mischief. Show yourself – stirrer of storms – the goad and the rider of Tormod."

"I said unarm yourself! And withdraw your men!"

"It is really you; I'd know your screech anywhere. The gods mock me," Rudolf said with a crack in his voice. He unbuckled his swordbelt and handed it to his nearest herse.

"You threatened to burn the house of God, and me inside!" the voice screamed out.

"The wrath of unwieldy Thor is within my wrist," Rudolf said. "The whetstone chips at my forehead. A misstep. And what, have you given yourself over to the White Christ?"

"I have!" the same woman inside shouted. "Now step back, you adulterous heathen!"

It sounds so much like her – have the Gods punished me? A frosty Hel to dance with her again!

Rudolf stood silent for a spell. He paced backward more, the banner-woman hooked his arm, and a kerchiefed head poked out from the church. She stood upright and walked out, two thick braids bouncing along her red-yellow long dress as she did. *Frida Two-Plait!*

"Frida," Rudolf said as he slipped a finger under the collar of his tunic. "I had not been forewarned of your presence here in Orkney!"

"And so I hear you have been bedding with some harlot!" she screamed out the last word, as forceful as a leather needle pierces a hide.

The banner-woman went asnarl as Rudolf's armsmen put a hand on her dainty shoulder. She stomped off.

"You were in Norway," he said, nonplussed. "What should I have done, if I am outlawed and banished to Orkney without my wife?"

"And to think I stayed faithful toward you for so many winters!"

"Yet your legs parted for a viking – the rider and goad of Tormod indeed," Rudolf said.

"I am no adulterer! Only after I found out you mounted some whore! Our marriage is split!"

"Many lonely nights I had in these windswept islands – I outlawed to this wasteland while you free in forested Norway."

Frida honked out a sob. "And do you know what happened to your son?!"

Rudolf's face went as grim as a mask.

"Beheaded!" she said with another sob. "I pray for his soul daily."

Rudolf's trembling hand wrapped his off-hand around the pommel of his sword, as if to crush it.

"Who?"

"The Jarl Haakon," she said, turned her head, and spat.

No, not Haakon. It may have been his sword, but I was the edge of his blade. I was Arild's death, and Rudolf will have my head for that.

"One of Finehair's puppies," Rudolf said.

Frida and eight cowled women set forth through the gawking onlookers.

"Still your feet," Rudolf said, "you have much to answer, Frida Two-Plait."

"Nay," Audun said as he emerged from the crowd. "I, as housecarl of Jarl Toke, grant her mercy. We do not need more trouble – let her leave Orkney."

"And what misjustice is this?" Rudolf asked. "My wife sleeps with a viking, goads him to raid, fights against the Jarl's men – and I am to let her wander off?"

"In the name of Jarl Toke. Men – wapentake if you agree!" Audun shouted.

Over half of the warriors beat their spearshafts against their shieldfaces. Asgeir went noiseless as Rudolf scanned the crowd. He found his silent Svears outnumbered, and Audun's men roused.

"It is settled – Frida Two-Plait, you are hereby banished from Orkney. Gather your belongings and find passage."

"Another besmirchment, another banishment – the heathen has no shame! I shall seek out Christian men, and live a Godly life, and the White Christ will reward me for it in Folkvangr!"

"Luck was with you today, Frida," Rudolf said. "May your soul wander in joyless Helheim, oathbreaker, figurehead of a viking's prow."

"And unluck to you, Rudolf High-Cheater!"

Rudolf and Frida turned their backs on one another. He walked off into the misty alleyways of the longhouses, and she and her handmaidens headed for the stairs.

Frida Two-Plait. Her hair parted in twain, a two-headed snake. Nothing but venom dribbles from those lips. She plotted to murder Ulf, which led to the sundering of Kjetil Redcloak's Rikheim. Even after Tyr meted out his justice, and her son paid it with his eye, she washed Haakon's Borgund in Arild's blood. As she urged her son and their kin and neighbors to strike Borgund in Norway, she surely armed Tormod. As sure as Thor fries trolls with his lightning, this Frida weaves war. A pock on you, Audun, for letting her go. I'd strike her down myself if I were lawman.

"Troubled times, son," Hallgeir said as he placed a hand on Asgeir's hunched shoulder. "Very troubled. Odin himself has stirred the storm. Let's set a gulf between these scorned lovers. There is much to discuss among father and son."

"I agree, father," he said. *But I have grim news for you.*

With his father's arm around his shoulders, Hallgeir led him across the sward of Birsay. Asgeir gazed at the visage of his father, in profile, his heavy-scarred brow, how his beard stayed crisp even after the tumult of wind and rain and battle. *Father, I beheaded Rudolf's son,* he thought. *Can I tell you that? You'd be ashamed of me, and Rudolf would bring his rage upon us. Yet I cannot live with this dishonesty.*

Asgeir and his father sat on a bench in the hall of Birsay, ringed by rows of warriors along the lit longhearth. Behind them, a pair spoke in an undertone about the absence of Jarl Toke. From what Asgeir eavesdropped, many suspected that Rudolf would claim the jarldom as his own, as he had many armed followers, several ships, and a long and proud lineage. The God Freyr, of bountiful peace, his eldest grandfather.

"There is much to discuss, Father," Asgeir said. "I've missed you terribly."

Hallgeir said nothing, but his smile eased and his eye cocked. "You have horrid news. A father knows."

"Yes, Father," Asgeir said. "By Njordr, I live. But Odd does not."

The eyes of his father dimmed.

"Ulf the Old came to Damsgaard – to collect his debt, he said. He demanded to take us on as sailors. We challenged him to holmgang, but we lost, and Odd was killed."

"Ulf the Old," Hallgeir said and hacked spit in the fire. It sizzled. "My eldest son – dead. By good Freyr."

Neither of them said anything for a long while. Asgeir went thoughtless; just the image of Odd's grayed face flickered in his mind.

"I will kill Ulf the Old," Hallgeir said after a time.

"He drowned."

They both went silent again.

"If you survived, how did he not?"

"I was on the ship with him when it went down. We were the last ones on board. The enemies took some of us prisoner. Ulf was not one of them."

"Then I am robbed of vengeance," Hallgeir said.

"As am I, Father," Asgeir said. "I swore revenge on him. I wanted to kill him myself."

"You?" Hallgeir said. "You'd be no match for him. He's always been crafty. Bah! I hate that I outlive Odd!"

I am not the same man as before the storm – or that blood-storm back at Borgund.

"Mother was in such pain," Asgeir said. "Auntie Bjorg hexed the ship. that's why it sank."

"I heard of that battle and sinking – you survived by your aunt's blessing, I am sure of it. But Ulf – tell me, does he have any living sons?"

"Yes, Rolf Ulfsson."

"Then I will kill Rolf Ulfsson."

"Father," Asgeir said. *I don't wish to press him in this moment of grief, that Rolf is my friend.* They both went silent for a long spell as the logs of the fire crackled.

Hallgeir smiled, though his eyes belied his grief. "Be merry, son. This life is short. Through it all, stay merry, laugh at death!"

"You're right. I've lived this long. I cannot even tell you what these months have brought me. The wheels of an unfastened axel on an uneven road!"

"And you are the better man for it," Hallgeir said. "I saw you in the battle today. You looked fierce." He drained a soapstone cup. "Yes, indeed, I am merry, despite my sadness. I will avenge Odd, if not through Ulf the Old, then by Rolf Ulfsson, for honor demands it! Indeed – I feel for that Rudolf High-Hat now, for no father should live without his son, and no killer of his son should go unavenged."

Before Asgeir could speak, a horn blew from outside. The murmurings of the crowd grew as the warriors funneled out of the gangways.

Asgeir followed his father toward the people that had gathered around the olden Pictish church. The wind howled as Rudolf High-Hat stood upon a heap of stones in the grass in front of the wrecked door of the church.

"Grave tides today," he said through a wooden loudhailer. "Odin has reaped his harvest, and all of Orkney's islands tilt toward ruin. Vikings dare to raid and pillage and rob Jarl Toke's land. Something was undreamed of in this realm when your forebears first arrived and vanished the Picts. Now what comes of it?

"Rumors of war – winds of change – greedy men driven by want of plunder. Jarl Toke's land is tarnished, and much weakness rears. These times call for a man of strength – tell me, is Jarl Toke strong?

"The crops of Orkney have withered. Vikings make much mischief. A tyrant weening-at-tit over in Norway threatens to rule you. Where is Jarl Toke?" He paused. "He's either dead or a coward, I'd say."

Some men gasped. A throng of Rudolf's warriors stood like guards, their yellow riding-coats wrapped around their sturdy torsos, spear-armed, and they beat their shafts against their shieldfaces to quiet the mutters.

"Shall you revolt against these words, men of Orkney?" Rudolf said. The sun hit the silver cone on his cap. "Shall you revolt against mere words, and not the weakness of your jarl? Tell me, then, where is Jarl Toke?"

The crowd quieted. Hallgeir tapped on Asgeir's shoulder and spoke low in his ear.

"He's right – and what balls to take up leadership on news of death of his son, and strife with his wife. I don't care what he did to get banished from Norway – that silver bit on his hat means he's Svear nobility, and it shows through his actions."

My father respects him – but what will he do when he knows it was I who beheaded Arild? I didn't want to – why was I so weak?

"If Harald sends forth his force, who will halt them? Will it be Jarl Toke? No. A poor ruler is unfit to rule. In Uppsala, we would hang him from an oak," Rudolf said as his face darkened. "You Nordmenn do not practice such. But I digress – you are all good, hardy men. You brave this foul weather on these stormbound isles like goats brave cliffs. You need a jarl, or you will get a king. I declare myself, Rudolf High-Hat, son of the Ynglings, the Jarl of Orkney."

His line of warriors beat their shields and cheered, and half the crowd cheered as well.

"If Toke Not-Jarl wishes to vie for the jarldom," Rudolf said, "then he may do so if he shows his worthless, pale hide to these islands."

More of the men cheered, and Asgeir winced when his father whistled hard.

"Let Tyr, God of justice, decide if I am fit to rule. I will swear an oath on Odin's gold ring to lead you, as my Yngling ancestors have led in Svearia since the golden age of heroes. And by the Grim-One," Rudolf said and unsheathed his sword. "If Jarl Haakon of Borgund, or any of the other puppies of Harald step one foot on our beaches – they will meet a tide of iron."

Hallgeir cupped his mouth like a loudhailer and chanted: *Rudolf!*

A chant sounded across Birsay. The warriors all slapped their shields in one fell din as they chanted "Rudolf! Rudolf! Rudolf!"

"Who would have thought the Svears would impress me?" Hallgeir asked his son with a wink. "They've got the crowd in their palms – me among them. This is the kind of man I'd follow to war."

Now the men all sang:

His twin cries amber tears,

The logs in his hearth sears.

His bounty and plentiful,
We strike for Freyr's will!
For if peace can only come through war,
The God of the Yngling rides his boar.

"I am Jarl Rudolf High-Hat, and Freyr of peace is with us. Tonight, we feast in his honor! And for the honor of my slain son – unjustly – Arild Rudolfsson."

Two He-Thralls rolled a barrel of ale across the sward. One handed Rudolf an axe. With his sword in one hand, he raised the axe overhead and smashed the barrel in twain. Brown-red water poured out and drenched the ground. Asgeir sniffed the air and knew it smelled like wine, the delight of the Romans. He had only tasted it once before but always remembered its sourness.

"And the second barrel to Freyr," Rudolf said as he heaved up his axe, but just tapped each stave with the butt-end. "For you to share with him."

The crowd ringed around the church as Rudolf passed a horn full of wine to each man.

"I only ask that you take one sip to Freyr, for the good, plenty, and peace of these fair islands."

Asgeir found his heart heavy, for he shared wine with the father of the man he slew on the ground, on behalf of Jarl Haakon. Halfway down the line, Rudolf refilled it, and Asgeir watched his father down more than a gulp.

"I haven't tasted wine since I was down in Ireland," Hallgeir said. "They think it's the blood of their God."

Asgeir took the horn, now marred with fingerprints, yet the silver along the rim sparkled. He took a sip and whispered "Freyr."

Arild – I did you wrong. Your father will take revenge on me, won't he? By the Gods – what a tangle.

Be merry.

"There is much catching up to do, Asgeir," Hallgeir said. "We throw our lot in with this Rudolf. Go on – enjoy the feast, plenty of pretty girls to snag. Let us meet later, I will ensure we get seated near Rudolf."

Hallgeir mussed Asgeir's hair and walked away. Asgeir turned to walk but Eirik grabbed hold of his arm. By the look in his forlorn eyes, he knew he thought of Drusticca.

"That Svear spoke a lot, but said nothing about Tormod," he said. "What of my sister, Asgeir? What of her? And why didn't you strike that rassragr down when he ran for his ship?"

"To do so would be dishonorable," Asgeir said.

Eirik went blank-faced. The fingers tightened on his forearm. "What dishonorable things does he to do Drusticca?"

He walked off, and Asgeir stood in the midst of the revel alone. With little to merrymake, he headed down the stairs of Birsay to the boathouses, where the tide had filled and floated the boats. *Drusticca – I wonder where she is. Was she on Tormod's ship? Did I really have to let that viking go free? I could have slain him, then and there, and avenged her. Maybe my honor wasn't as important then.* He found Eirik's faering and there, Svartganger poked his head above the gunwale. Asgeir climbed up on board. Svartganger weaved between his shins as he leaned down to pet him. Asgeir rubbed his belly and the cat purred.

"You haven't seen Father in a while – he'll be so happy to see you."

Asgeir rolled out a fleece on the deck at the foot of his rowlock. He leaned his head against his chest as Svartganger settled between his legs. The purr of cat along the lull of the ocean sank him into a dream.

He found himself staring up, as a baby. He wished to turn over, but no strength allowed him. Two faces stood over him. His mother, Aelfrida, and his father, Hallgeir. Their smiles glowed as they leaned their heads together. His father jangled something above him – a necklace of pearls. Amber, jet, ivory. Asgeir tried to grab them, but had no arm-length to reach. His parents spoke, but he hadn't the ears to hear them.

His mother cradled him close to her bosom as his father vanished into the mist. Soon he found himself walking upright, and then, running through a forest, and swimming in a red-brown sea. The tears of Freya? His eyes closed as he sank into the amber.

He opened his eyes, and found himself on dry ground, but faced two cats harnessed. He followed the hitch of the harness, and there a chariot stood on a paved road. A chariot, the likes of which his forebears rode, only sung of in the old heroic poems.

Upon the cart, the most beautiful woman stood. Asgeir found her beauty so strong that he it was indescribable. She had flaxen hair but that was all Asgeir could fathom.

"Freya of the Dis and the Vanir. You've come to me!"

A cloak of feathers wrapped around her as she flew away, wordless.

"Come back, I need your guidance."

A warm hand took hold of his. Someone spun him, and he found himself face-to-face with an older woman. She had dark blond in a single plait, and dressed much in the manner of married ladies, with two oval-shaped brass brooches over an apron-like dress. She smiled warmly, motherly wrinkles garnished her face. She kissed his forehead as he turned to look toward Freya.

"Listen not to her, my child, for I am Frigga, and I have the gift of foresight," the other woman said.

"Frigga, wife of Odin, you've come to me now."

"Walk with me, and there will be no regrets or guilt."

His nose throbbed as someone's lips touched his. A seal played in the wavelets on Rousay's strand. It washed ashore, stood upon its hind-fins, raised a flipper to its head and drew a string. Its skin slumped around the ankles of a slim, ivory-skinned, raven-haired girl. *Fina.* She approached him, barking like a seal, and kissed his lips. Dry, soft, cold. *Fina, I'll never forget your kiss, but I have a duty to your brother. Eirik, I lost Drusticca, I failed you as a watchman.*

Asgeir awoke.

Two goddesses visited me in that dream. What meaning did it hold? Frigg said she has foresight, and to not listen to Freya. Do they quarrel, like we do here on Midgard?

Something pressed his lips and startled him. Svartganger's eyes widened, spooked, and Asgeir followed the cat's gaze. Someone jumped off the karve's deck and splashed through the water. He seized a stray spear from the deck and rushed over, yet found nothing but wavelets. Onboard, a rug rolled off a chest and unraveled, splayed out among the sitting-chests.

Someone's been onboard, looking through our things! Or perhaps the sidhe – or my fylgja, Nosey? Either way, I'd best get back to the feast. He scooped up Svartganger and headed back to the noisy fort.

Asgeir braced against the howling wind as he trekked toward the hall, where the feast must have been raging for the last few hours. The door, carved in Pictish beasts in the Pictish manner, opened and Asgeir found his father there. He raised his eyebrows.

"Asgeir – where've you been? I was just about to look for you."

"Sleeping, Father. The days have been full of battle."

"Svartganger?"

Hallgeir scratched the cat along his muzzle until he jumped down and brushed against his legs.

"I never thought I'd see that cat again! Come on, Asgeir – Odin honors us, we are seated next to the High-Seat of the Jarl!"

Hallgeir wore a long white linen tunic, knee-length, and nothing else save for a fringed red cloak wrapped around his body many times, and a red silk headband. Asgeir thought he dressed somewhat Irish.

"Have you no clothing for the feast? You're the son of the Huskarl, after all."

"Nay, Father," he said, "my feasting clothes went down with the Sea-Bitch."

Hallgeir unlatched a comb of antler by his belt, and ran it through Asgeir's hair. From a small leather pouch, he sprinkled some small herbs about his son's collar. "You are awfully underdressed my son. Come."

In the smoky hall, three long tables with nine warriors each spanned the length. At the end, Rudolf sat on a wooden chair bedecked in strange beastly carvings, his mistress and another woman seated next to him. Audun sat down next to them, attempting to join the conversation, but Rudolf cast him a glance and said, "You're in the wrong seat, Audun Seven-Fingers."

"I'm the housecarl to Jarl Toke," he said.

Rudolf pointed further down the table. Audun jutted his jaw, and his white beard ruffled as he lumbered away. Passing Asgeir, his shoulder brushed his, and the might of the beastly old war-walker knocked him off balance.

Hallgeir sat and beckoned Asgeir to sit down between he and a smiling woman. She had shoulder-length brown hair, and greeted him with a wave from underneath her walnut-dyed cloak.

"Welcome to the feast, son of Hallgeir," she said with a twang he didn't know.

Hallgeir took his seat and Asgeir sat among them. After a puzzled look, Hallgeir said, "this is my wife, Godifu."

Asgeir just hung there. "Your wife? But Mother is your wife."

His father let out a peal of laughter. Godifu blushed but rolled her eyes.

"Well, we call it the way of the Danes in my country," she said.

"Father," Asgeir said. "Does Mother know?"

"She'll know someday, perhaps. Asgeir, do you know how I met Godifu? It was on a raid down in Skottland. She was taken captive by the Skotts – she's from Northumbria in Angeland."

"I've heard so much about you, Asgeir," she said. "You're tall and handsome, like your father."

"Not halfway as much as I, yet," Hallgeir said and let out another peal of laughter.

"Asgeir, I heard you braved the North Sea in winter," she said. Before Asgeir could think or say anything, she continued. "Have you been told about your brother?"

"My brother? Odd?"

"No, not him. Poor lad, I would have loved to have met him. Our son, Aelfsige! He's been fostered down in Angeland, by a Kentish king."

Another brother? Father, it's been too many years. I barely know you at all.

"Forgive me, Godifu," Asgeir said, "and Father, but I am unsure what to make of this."

Hallgeir slapped him on the shoulder so hard that his wine cup spilled over his fingers. Godifu leaned over and dabbed it up with a rag.

"We planned to venture down south to Angeland to find my son, as a messenger on behalf of the King of Lothlend. I owe that Kentish king – he gifted me this sword! We journeyed here just to haven in Birsay – maybe eat some puffin – but Father War has me feeding the crows!" Hallgeir said with another gusty laugh.

"Asgeir," Rudolf High-Hat said. The firelight from the longhearth behind him danced, lighting his fine coat, and its bedazzling kingly silver. "I've heard that you were at the battle of Borgund."

All eyes turned toward him, as if he were a singing skald who recants the deeds of kings and heroes and gods through song. Rudolf, his mistress, his father, and Godifu. His father, chief among them, lifted his eyebrows and nodded. *He wants to hear the story, but I am in no mood to tell it. And Helvete! I don't want Rudolf to know it was I who killed Arild.*

"I was there, it was a hard battle, and many men died," Asgeir said as he yanked his tunic down to show his healing spear wound. "I was stabbed hard, but by the grace of Saga's healing hand."

"Saga the Healer?" Hallgeir asked. "Lucky man – you will yet live then! I wouldn't mind her hands on me – spear wound or not!" He laughed but found a glare from Godifu, and put a hand to his mouth. "But the battle – my son, wounded by spear in the shieldwall! Come on, tell Rudolf about the battle."

"Forget the battle. Tell me about Arild, Asgeir."

"What do you mean, gracious host?"

"I have heard that Jarl Haakon slew my son," Rudolf said.

Rudolf's brow deepened. All Asgeir could muster was a nod.

"How did my son come to be on the edge of Haakon's sword?"

"Arild led an attack on Haakon's hall," Asgeir said as he quenched the memory of Sakka's white, lithe body from his mind.

"That I heard," Rudolf said, his wine cup now midway to his mouth. "Tell me how he died, I wish to know how it came to be."

Asgeir stumbled over his words. Rudolf peered at him.

"Before he died," Asgeir said, and Rudolf's eyes shone at the thought. "He said that his mother had put him up to it."

"That worthless hag!" the blond mistress of Rudolf said. "Urged her own son, sounds like her!"

"True or untrue," Rudolf said as he swirled the wine in his hand, "it was not Frida that beheaded him. She loved him as any mother. Haakon saw to his death, and I will see that Haakon's head rides my spear."

He's dogging me. He knows there's more to it. I've slipped up, but I cannot outright lie.

"Asgeir, when they blemished Midgard with such a misdeed – where were you, if you were injured?"

"Close to the battleline, and they spoke loudly," he said. "The enemy line collapsed shortly after the spear struck me, and we won." Asgeir squirmed in his seat.

"You seem uncomfortable," Rudolf said.

"It was a hard battle – it shakes me to think of it. My unreadiness caused the death of my friend, Erle, our captain."

Asgeir could feel his father frown.

"What he means is that his wound hurts. Isn't that right, Asgeir?"

"It does, Father."

A cold, small hand rubbed circles on his shoulder. He found Godifu smiling, her lips puckered, much like a mother tending her child. She brandished a small brass pendant of a club from around her neck, as if to heal his wound with it. *You're not my mother, woman.*

"My son was not foolish," Rudolf said. "Surely, Frida must have rallied her allies by anger or outrage, for very few men would attack the hall of a Jarl by rally of more than her word."

Still Asgeir said nothing, but Rudolf continued.

"How did you come to feast at Borgund?"

"Ulf the Old – he coerced me to sail with him."

"Ulf the Old – Frida hates him even more than I do," Rudolf said. "That Ulf the Old is scum. No good eggs lay from the ass of an ill hen. Yes, I am sure his presence in Laerdal wrought the hatred of Frida and her allies upon Haakon."

That's not untrue – but by Tyr, God of justice, I feel dirty for this. I can scarcely look the man in the eyes. It should have been Frida there, on her knees and under the blade.

His eyes met Rudolf's. His chest clenched.

"And Ulf the Old is dead, I have heard. Is this true?"

"Drowned. He murdered a Pict portman, and Audun and his men overcame us."

"Good."

"Ulf drowned?" Hallgeir said with a growl. "It looks like neither of us will get justice, Rudolf."

Rudolf drained his wine and placed the Frankish-crafted cup down, staring at it.

"You fought as bravely at Birsay as you did at Borgund, I hear. You are your father's son. The courage of others fell, while yours stood. A sea stack against the ocean."

"Worthy praise for my son, and for me, as his father, Rudolf. If true to your words, then you should reward him."

"Hardships come," Rudolf said, "but they are short. A day of war will be followed by a year of peace. I will reward you, but you must fight for me, Asgeir."

Asgeir brought himself to look into the iron-gray eyes of Rudolf.

I freed myself from the yoke of Ulf and found my father. But fight for Rudolf? How could I?

"Jarl Toke was loved before he vanished. It's summer's start, and if Toke lives, Orkney will foreknow his return. Then the farmers will revolt against you," Hallgeir said.

"Some of them, yes. Some will join Tormod. Many will die – ours and theirs. When you slay a wolf, what takes his den? Another wolf. We will be that wolf, Asgeir."

"You forethink men to die, so others may take their land?" Asgeir asked.

"Don't you know about my father?" Hallgeir said and put an arm around him. "Your grandfather had the same as in Eigg! Neither the Pictish chiefs nor the Gaelic monks could match him and his sea-wolves!"

"But we have land – on Eigg, and at Damsgaard."

"Damsgaard? You must forget about Norway," Hallgeir said to Asgeir. "Harald will see to it that we cannot live without his tethers. And Eigg – don't worry about our farm there. It's in tender hands. You'll be happy on Orkney. We'll find you a proper lady."

"I have cousins in Angeland you could meet," Godifu said with a wink to him.

"No need, my love, Asgeir will have the pick of widows here."

Asgeir's mind jittered like a wayward boat. His father and Rudolf spoke, but he just sat there, a sturdy post, with neither sense nor thought.

Hallgeir put a hand on his son's shoulder. Asgeir sat up and looked straight. "You will have the pick of the widows," Hallgeir said again.

"There will be plunder, and land, and women," Rudolf said. "Orkney will be scourged like Angeland under the Danes."

"Ah the Danes – so handsome they are," Godifu said. She fluttered her eyelashes in a swoon.

"Not as much as the Nordmenn! I've proven that!" Hallgeir said and laughed as he slapped Asgeir hard on the back.

Rudolf lowered his gaze to his cup as a Pict refilled it.

"My son was handsome."

He said nothing more, but Asgeir knew what he thought. As the people with the so-called *sight* down in the Skottland and Ireland who could read thoughts, he knew. Rudolf thought of his son, how his handsome face grayed, and what sort of burial someone deemed a criminal would receive – nothing save for the carrion eaters. The realm of Hel awaited him, a solemn and somber place, without the revelry of Valhal or Folkvangr. Better than Helheim, where oathbreakers and murderers and those men of dishonor faced everlasting disgrace. But never mind Valhal, where a warrior like Arild deserved. Never mind the vagrant on his knees under the blade, for Odin had demanded death for treason. No, not Odin – Haakon.

Rudolf leaned his head back and closed his eyes, as if he basked in the sun.

By Odin, Haakon, you coward! You had me kill him so someone else would take Rudolf's vengeance!

"Asgeir, how did he die?" Rudolf asked again.

Asgeir sat alert.

"Did he laugh, as Ragnar in the snake pit? Did he declare that he looked forward to dining with his friends, as King Radbad of Frisia? Did he declare it his time to die?"

Asgeir saw Arild on his hands and knees like a whore, pleading for his life underneath the man who he once joined in the warrior-walk.

"I haven't the foggiest. My spear wound was too grave for me to remember."

I hate that I lie. To a man's face, and in front of my father. But I couldn't bear to tell him that his son died sniveling and begging. It should be Haakon telling him this.

Rudolf just stared back at him, his heart not unwounded, but his eyes falcon-like, focused on Asgeir.

"I will carve the eagle on the back of whoever killed him."

"It was Jarl Haakon," Asgeir said, and understood he spoke too quickly.

The wise man keeps silent, says the High One.

Someone burst into the hall and raced toward Rudolf. The Svear stood up at attention. The man, a youth with a budding mustache, had a puffy flushed face and spat out his words.

"Rudolf – I am sorry but – it's Tormod."

Rudolf clasped the hilt of his sword and pivoted to raise a hand to his roused warriors.

"No," the watchman said, "he's not attacking – he's surrendered!"

With a hand still on his hilt, Rudolf rushed out of the hall. His men followed, and in the muggy outdoors, Asgeir found a man kneeling somber on the sward of Birsay.

The vikings wore just their soiled linen undertunics. A pile of glinting metal lay before them, axes and spears and one sword, and many silver coins under nicked ingots. Tormod presented a leg o' lamb on a platter before it.

"I see we have brought you to a grovel," Rudolf said, and in three steps, stood over Tormod.

Tormod met his gaze, his eyes glassy, his lip furled.

"You would never surrender on your own goodwill," Rudolf said. "I know youth like you, and you are too proud for humility. Who forced you here?"

"Frida Two-Plait," Tormod said. "She swayed our minds with her tongue."

"Her tongue oftentimes does lick," Rudolf said with a sneer. "Go on."

"She told us that our Gods abandoned us, and that is why we lost. That we would starve this winter. Here." He nudged the wooden platter of roast piglet toward Rudolf. "A gesture of goodwill. The last salted meat from my home. And weapons. And silver. I beg that you spare our lives, for we were just hungry."

"Frida stayed true to her word to leave Orkney?"

"Yes, she left for Skottland. To seek a church. She said she will marry her God. She said she would not travel with heathens, and urged us to surrender."

"This early in the year, crossing the Pent Sound, in this wind. She'll marry Aegir's daughters. Good riddance."

With a hand on the polished-antler handle of his sword, Rudolf gazed down at Tormod. He turned to the men of Birsay.

"I hereby call for a judgment. Let us not wait for the next Thing moot, let Tyr deal his justice today. The law demands death for rapists, plunderers, criminals. Shall these vikings die?"

The crowd roared. Asgeir too, among them. *Tormod deserves it – taking Drusticca like she was booty. Midgard needs less criminals like him, hungry or not.*

Rudolf turned toward Tormod and his vikings. They all sat silent. Tormod rose to his feet and bowed his head, his sunburnt neck the offering. Rudolf gripped his sword-hilt hard, his red-leather scabbard lifted on its brass-ring baldric.

The snake-sound, when the sword draws from its scabbard, never sounded. The sword stayed in its scabbard like a worm stubborn and snug in its hole. A cowled woman gasped.

"Orkney must follow its own laws – not the law of Harald and his Nordmenn. Tyr decides it. Tyr has spoken it. The hand of Tyr stayed," Rudolf said.

"No," Eirik said as he elbowed forward through the crowd. "There's no lack of weapons – kill him by his own axe!"

Rudolf said nothing in response as he unhooked the clasp of his swordbelt and his wargear thudded to the ground.

"The God of justice has spoken. Tyr rebukes my sword, thus Tormod lives. The God's wapentake has declared him a hostage for his kin to buy. For such a misdeed, the Orkney folk should have flame-farewelled him, yet the Gods have spoken today."

Tormod seized a small silver ring from the loot pile and brandished it to Rudolf. Both men pinched either side and tugged at one another, to swear an oath.

Eirik opened his mouth and raised his grizzled arm, but Asgeir grabbed hold of it and pulled it down. "You need to relax," Asgeir said. With a hand on his shoulder, Asgeir dragged him from the frontline of people. Eirik scrunched up his face at Asgeir, ripped himself away, and stomped off. Asgeir followed him into the alleyway of two longhouses.

"Drusticca goes unavenged after what that fucking viking did to her, and where is she?" Eirik said as his sweaty, calloused hand tugged his arm.

"The sword refused to leave its sheath," Asgeir said.

"The air is fucking moist! The scabbard's sheepskin just got thicker – don't you know the one thing I fucking know is sheep?" Eirik said and tugged harder.

Asgeir's vision reddened when his spear wound flared, and he shoved Eirik hard into the stone-wall of the longhouse. That winded him. Eirik wheezed but writhed.

"Don't you think I hate that bastard too for what he has done to Drusticca?" Asgeir said as he held Eirik against the longhouse.

"She's my fucking sister – let me go!"

The whetstone of Thor, the whetstone in his head, it makes him rash, wrathful, his weakness.

Eirik lost balance and slid to the ground as Asgeir backed away. When he got to his feet, he brushed some dust off his beige trousers and stamped down the alley.

"What of our friendship?" Eirik said as he left.

"I should have stopped Tormod, at least found out where Drusticca was," Asgeir said to Eirik, but he didn't turn back.

Asgeir returned to the mead-hall, and drank the last draft of the bitter wine, unbeknownst to him how it tasted, for nerves masked even the bitterest taste. The Pict slave refilled his cup, the bounty of Freyr, God of peace, mirthful as it flowed, and Asgeir found himself led out of the hall with his father. By the look on his face, he knew his father had much to discuss with him.

CHAPTER VI

The Goddess of Peace

The steam stung his eyes as he found himself in the bathhouse. His father sat across from him, leaned back. The paved stone floor burned Asgeir's bare feet, and he coughed from the smoke of the hot coals.

"The steam clears one's nose, one's throat, one's mind," Hallgeir said. "And it is as clear as a Midsummer's eve what must be done. I always thought hatred would boil in me if someone killed one of my sons. But I am joyous, because I will have revenge."

"But Ulf is dead, father."

"His son is not."

Asgeir bit his lip. "Rolf joined at his father's command. He cannot be blamed."

A bare-chested slave entered and poured water from a jug into the center of the bathhouse. A wisp of steam rose and thickened. Asgeir averted his gaze, but Hallgeir shoved his face into it with a laugh. Asgeir wrestled out, and shoved his father forward, into the thick of the steam as he coughed. They both laughed.

"Blood must spill for Odd," Hallgeir said after they had silenced.

"Rolf Ulfsson is my friend, Father."

"No," Hallgeir said.

"It was Ulf, Father. Rolf just obeyed him."

"What does Rolf offer you?"

"Offer me?"

"Your friends must offer you something, and you them. It is like the gods. We offer them gifts, they offer us gifts. We give them treasure, beasts, and mead. They give us cleverness, guidance, wisdom. What does Rolf offer you?"

Asgeir said nothing for a spell as his sweat simmered on the stone bench.

"He was there for me, Father, during the storm off Hjaltland, and the siege at Borgund. He offers me friendship."

Hallgeir laughed. "You have much to learn in life, my son. You've grown gullible, and we must change that, for there are many wolves like Ulf roaming."

"I'm not, Father," he said. "I have seen the Gods in dreams, and they guide me, as I listen to them."

Hallgeir stroked his hairy chin. "Of course, we are children of the Gods. They advise their children. Odin is our eldest forefather, and you should listen to his advice. You must choose your friends wisely, and then your enemies will choose you unwisely. And never marry a woman for love."

"Then why get married?"

Hallgeir pealed out a laugh. "Love is for your mistress. Marriage is for your ambitions. And as Godifu says, the way of the Danes will allow your ambitions to come to fruition!"

"Mother never agreed to that. But Father," Asgeir thought to switch the conversation, for he did not wish to cause strife between his parents, "what did you owe to Ulf?"

Hallgeir leaned his sweat-drenched head back.

"In the early days of Lothlend, Ulf and I were vikings in liege of the Sea-King. We lived in his ship. We ate mightily and took what we wanted and had much to be merry about. One summer, we sailed to Dubh Linn to trade, before we would harry the Irish and Welsh. When we passed by the thrall market, I found the loveliest woman I had ever seen. Now, I was just a whelp then, without much wealth to me, but I wanted her. Her master said she was an Irish princess, and I needed much silver for her. Ulf lent it to me, for we were friends, and I promised to pay him back. She is your mother."

Why didn't you pay him back? If you had, Odd would have been alive.

I can't just say that – he's as grieved as I am.

And my mother? A slave? And a princess? Father, you've been reckless.

A slender silhouette entered the steamy bath. A woman with frizzy black hair hauling a too-heavy jug squatted down next to the firestones and poured. The jug slipped from her hand and cracked on the stone floor. She giggled at her own clumsiness as she picked up the pieces. After a shy glance at Asgeir, she hurried out, he caught a whiff of seawater, and Asgeir knew her as Fina.

"Fina? Is that you?"

"Eyefuls," Hallgeir said with a laugh. "You take after me after all! Pretty one and she seemed to like you! Go on then – it's very much too hot in here now, anyway. Go on after her, and conquer, son."

He stood up and stretched and left, and another familiar figure entered. Tormod and Asgeir came face-to-face, both staring. The sweat poured down Asgeir's back and wettened his hair above the ears.

"Tormod," Asgeir said. "Where is Drusticca? She'd best be unharmed."

Tormod narrowed his eyes. "She left Orkney. Frida Two-Plait adopted her as a handmaiden. I will say nothing further. Rudolf has me hostage, and allowed me a night of rest, for we have a truce."

"Truce or not, Tormod, your dirtiness in that duel will haunt you."

"If you wish for another duel, that can be arranged," he said, "if the Gods stay my death."

"Not to the death – just the first cut," Asgeir said, "since Orkney should know peace."

"Then let us arrange it at the Thing," Tormod said.

"I agree."

Both men stepped away from each other. Asgeir left the steam-house to the fore chamber where he toweled himself dry. As he clothed himself, a thud pounded in the bathhouse.

Footsteps raced out from the steam-house as Tormod stumbled toward him. He held his belly, where red holes pocked him like the seams of a shoe. He gasped and moaned a "help" as he collapsed to the stone floor, his face bouncing off the pavement. More red holes speckled his back. When he flipped over, his hand slid off his belly to reveal countless gashes. A broken piece of a jug handle was lodged in his groin.

"Helvete!" Asgeir cried.

Two young men stood at the entrance. They piled in and dragged Tormod up in a trail of blood. He still drew breath when they leaned him against a stone bench, but his eyes were glassed over, and he quaked in death-throes.

"Who did this?" the first youth said. Asgeir remembered him from the fight at Jarl Toke's farm, due to his steep browridge. That browridge furrowed harder at Asgeir.

Before Asgeir could say a word, the slender figure of a girl ghosted into the bathhouse, overjoyed at the sight of the quivering Tormod.

"I have done it," she said, a shard of ceramic still in her hand. "To think, they allowed that rassragr to rest! I snuck and sneaked and stealthed like the trickster until it was time to kill! I avenged Drusticca!"

Asgeir had to blink several times, for Fina stood there, a phantom of a girl in a gray dress splattered in blood.

"I told you I'd stab him," she acknowledged Asgeir with a laugh. "I told you I'd stab him to death!"

She thrust the shard through the air as the two men approached her. Asgeir found fieriness in their eyes. He stepped between the girl and Tormod's men, careful not to turn his back on the mad lass.

"Don't hurt her," Asgeir said. "Let the lawman judge her."

The two men glanced at each other and stepped forward.

"We must have order in Orkney, or Harald will come for us. Murderer may she be, let her have the judgment of Tyr, as Tormod had."

Fina slunk away out of the bathhouse as the two men went after her. Asgeir followed out into the benighted islet.

Uproar simmered in the fringe of longhouses along the southside of Birsay. Across the sward, Asgeir went opposite the fleeing sheep. He crossed the hill, the wind hard in his face, and when he wiped the wetness away, he found the shadow of Fina flitting by the cliff at the northside of the isle.

She must have hidden in Eirik's ship – in that carpet! It was her who dove into the water in the boathouse!

Even in the brine-breeze, she stunk of blood, odor, and seawater. She stood silent at the edge of the cliff, swaying with the wind. She heard him approach and turned her unkempt head toward him.

"Fina – I know why you did that, but it was still murder!"

She said nothing, she just swayed, her toes dancing on the very ledge of the cliff.

He took a step forward.

"You had no love for him, Asgeir, son of Hallgeir!"

"We agreed to settle it by duel, Fina. By the law. Whatever he did to your sister, the law would have settled it."

"Would it?" she said with a thick twang. She turned to him. He was taken aback when he spotted the long, sharp piece of pot clutched at her breast. "You Nordmenn speak the laws. You Nordmenn make us follow your laws. You Nordmenn decide who is guilty and who is innocent."

With a flick of her wrist, she brandished the pot piece, and cast it over the cliffside.

"A sidhe came to me in a dream," she said in Pictish, "and girded me with a sword. When I drew it, it screamed for vengeance, and could not be sheathed until it drank blood. It drank blood." She spoke more, but he didn't understand too much.

Asgeir found no words, for he knew that sword as Tyrfing. A living blade that must shed blood after it unsheathes.

"The sidhe call me home now," she said, and gazed down from the cliff. "They call me down there to jump. It is a better fate than what your people have for me."

She reached down to her ankles and yanked her dress over her head. The wind caught it and it fluttered away as she danced nude in the starlight. Asgeir took a few more steps toward her. *I can't let her jump. I don't know what they will do to her after she murdered him, but I still cannot let her die that way. I just can't bear it.*

"I'm a slave no longer. No Nordmann owns me. I shall become a selkie!"

With a hunched head, Fina crept up to Asgeir like a suspicious cat. She clasped his wrists and leaned up and kissed him, and barked like a seal. "Join me in the sea, Asgeir, and you too will live forever, in fairyland!"

Fina stepped backward off the ledge. In one bound, Asgeir dove on his belly and leaned over the cliff's lip. He grabbed her by the upper-arm. She let out a shriek as he hugged her. She dangled there as the strain on his thews shot through him and he found himself dragged toward the ledge. She rioted and kicked her legs.

"Please, Fina," he said, "don't fall!"

"Let me loose! Hel awaits!"

He felt a hand hold fast to his ankle and drag him away from the cliff. Asgeir found his father, heaving. When Fina crested the ledge, her arm hung and flapped loose as she shrieked, a thread without stitches. Once she was dragged up, he held her down and she cried.

Many footfalls across the sward made him aware that more had followed, probably by her shriek.

"Good work, son," Hallgeir said, "she will face justice now."

"I hope she is granted mercy," Asgeir said, "for Tormod has wronged her more than she him."

"I doubt Rudolf allows him to live for cuckoldry – but we'll see if the lawman sees that," Hallgeir said. He parted them. He took the girl's arm and shoved it back into the socket in a wet crack as she belted out a scream. His father then lifted the shivering girl into his mountainous form.

Fina, you utter fool. Drusticca deserved better, but so did you.

"My son, Asgeir, has apprehended this criminal," Hallgeir said as he set her down. She slumped to her knees, holding her wounded shoulder.

The crowd parted for Rudolf and his armsmen.

Rudolf stared featureless as he looked down on the girl. She didn't meet his gaze, but Rudolf gestured toward Asgeir. It reminded him of the way Haakon demanded him to deal out justice, and he shivered at that.

"You witnessed the murder and caught the murderer."

"Let me bear witness at the Thing," Asgeir said, "or else we will all be judged as lawless vikings."

"We shall put her before Tyr, God of justice, at first light," Rudolf said.

With an arm under each of hers, two men dragged the girl off back toward the longhouses. As the crowd dispersed, Rudolf gestured toward Asgeir and Hallgeir, then pointed toward his hall.

"You've done good work tonight," Hallgeir said as he placed a hand on his son's shoulder. "Rudolf looks even more favorably on you now. He is someone who ought to be our friend. Come, he invited us to sit near the high seat again."

Asgeir looked up at his father. The moonlight brightened his gray-streaked hair. Hallgeir smiled at him. *Rudolf will never befriend me once he finds out what I did to his son. But how can I tell my father?*

The nude, tousled form of Fina slipped away into the cram of the longhouse alleys. *That poor lass.*

CHAPTER VII

The Lawman of Orkney

The candlelight dappled Rudolf as he sat on the seat of honor in the hall of Birsay. Many men sat there, now after midnight, some still sipping the sour wine. Rudolf's woad-dyed hat looked like the dawning sky, with the silver stud ablaze like the morning star. Each of the brass buttons on his coat flickered. Asgeir spied the silk around the cuffs of his sleeves. He was a rich man, and his never-smiling face loosened.

"The Gods have robbed me. My son, beheaded. My wife – in her grief – has gone mad, bedded a viking, worships the nailed God rather than the hammerer, and ended our marriage. Yet I have been bestowed upon in my life with much. I step over each ditch in my way. I lean, but never fall. The Gods love brave men, who are cheerful with life. I take this cheerfulness in my grief. I refuse to allow my enemies conquest over me. Just when Freyr himself delivers peace at my doorstep, the fury of war, Odin, drags it away."

Asgeir fingered the sword hilt of Gael-Kisser. "Fina told me she had a dream that a sidhe, a troll that the Picts here believe in, gave her a sword that cannot be sheathed until it slays someone."

"The legend of Tyrfing," Rudolf said. "Yes, Odin is the God of the greater good. The all-plan. He makes no move without thinking ahead thrice. Neither will I."

Hallgeir patted the pommel of Gael-Kisser at Asgeir's waist. For a moment, Asgeir found Tyrfing sitting there in his scabbard. *It must drink blood.*

"The first step: the girl murdered someone. She must be punished. The second step: the free-men of Orkney may not believe the story – a Pictish thrall-girl murdered a full-grown man with a broken pot, rather than a cloaked murder by Rudolf High-Hat? They would think me the culprit, or at least, the stirrer of death. The third step: that Tormod the Colorless was the bastard son of Harvaard Greenfinger, the brother of Jarl Haakon of Borgund."

Asgeir caught something in his throat at the mention of Haakon. He sat there in the hall, alone, with just the must of the revelers still lingering who had been ferried out, and the stale wine of the uncleaned cups.

"Harvaard too was banished to Orkney, nine winters ago. Last year, he drowned on a fishing trip. Haakon never knew his bastard, but he will surely take for kin, in the name of his family's honor."

Hallgeir rubbed his belly as he slipped a scrap of chicken out of a bowl and slurped it down. "Then he should take revenge on the Pictish girl. Keep her alive, and hand her over to him."

"I will not parley with that scoundrel," Rudolf said. "Haakon murdered my son without trial. We cannot trust him. His mind changes as swift as winds, as steep as tides."

Hallgeir grunted. "No, that's not how it's done. If we are to show Harald that we islanders can fend for ourselves, then we need to follow our own laws. Hand the girl over to him. I can attend her to Laerdal – I have no quarrels with him or any in Norway."

"No, Father," Asgeir said, "I believe Rudolf is right. We saved Haakon's hall – we, the crew of the Sea-Bitch – and he still demanded that we leave after, ungratefully. I don't think we can trust him."

Hallgeir slammed his fist on the table. "No! You're both wrong, and the Gods will punish us for it!"

"My good friend, Hallgeir," Rudolf said. "You are a guest in my hall, may I remind you. The lord of hosts frowns upon the ill-mannered."

Hallgeir's face reddened. "Ill-mannered? I'll tell you – this is horseshit! Hand her over to the next-of-kin to Tormod."

"You have had much to drink – you slur your words," Rudolf said and Asgeir heard a slur in his too. "Listen to me, Hallgeir. We deal with this ourselves. We prove to the freemen of Orkney that Tormod was murdered as he has been – by a scorned Pictish thrall-girl – because of the rape of her sister. We will do so through a court with many witnesses."

"And Haakon will still scourge us for this."

"It will not be me as lawspeaker," Rudolf. "He will think I took revenge for my son. No. I will choose a lawspeaker who has no blood relation to either party."

"This is a mistake," Hallgeir said.

"I shall hear no more, Hallgeir, you have become annoying." Rudolf looked at Asgeir, his blue eyes aglow in candlelight. "Asgeir, you have shown responsibility today. You have a knack for the law, and you shall be my lawman."

"Me? A lawspeaker?" Asgeir said. His hand stiffened around his wine-cup.

"He's too young," Hallgeir said. "Like me or not, he's not suited for it. Or ready for it. But I am."

"Rudolf, I am undeserving of this."

"Nonsense," Rudolf said. "You saved the girl from the frothing mob – and called upon the law to do so. You are natural. Yes, tempered. I see much of my son, Arild, in you."

See your son in me? Helvete, Rudolf.

"Nevertheless," Hallgeir said with a voice like a commander, "I will support you, my son, and be ever proud. I know Odin will guide you to make the right decision."

"Then it is settled," Rudolf said. "In three days, you will be the lawspeaker and will judge the Pict girl. Yes, a hanging in the morning to start the new day of the new Jarl. I am sure you will make the right judgment."

If only my father had been quieter – he would have been the lawspeaker, not me. No, I must not whine about my fate – as Eirik said. I will grant justice to Fina.

After a spell of silence, Rudolf placed a silver-ringed hand on Asgeir's.

"Now I ask you to leave me for my ponderings. I suggest you do the same, Asgeir."

Asgeir and Hallgeir left the hall while Rudolf leaned his head back, muttering a prayer to Freyr over his Frankish-crafted wine cup.

Outside, the mist lowered over the bloodied strand and father and son stood under the starlit sky. Freya's distaff, the string of three stars, caught his eye first. *Freya, you watch me. You guide me. Speak to me again.*

"Father, there is something I must tell you. It eats at me. I must say that I have no honor."

"Go on," Hallgeir said with a glare.

"I was so weak at the battle of Borgund. I shirked from the fight and that killed Erle, my commander. Then … when Arild was defeated, Haakon, well…" Asgeir looked around to ensure no one listened. "He demanded that I kill Arild. I was the one to slay him."

"So Haakon could defer the lawless deed to you."

"I didn't want to do it. He was on his knees. I know … I know you said no man deserves to die like that. But I killed him. Haakon said Odin demanded it."

"The thoughts of Rudolf – that he must think steps ahead of his enemies. He thought that some of the blame would be put on you – and rightfully so. Now those who will feud for his blood may come for you."

"You're going to tell him," Asgeir said as if in relief.

"No, I would never do that to my son," Hallgeir said. "I am afraid Haakon has played us well, and Rudolf will be angrier with you than him. But Rudolf plays us well – it will be you who judges the murderer of his nephew, not him, Asgeir. And perhaps he hopes Haakon will venge upon you instead. This is Haakon's fault for forcing you to do it, and he shall pay for it. But do you not know why I became so disagreeable? I didn't want this on you – Rudolf was honest when he said he was three steps ahead of Haakon. Those dueling Jarls caught you by one ball each, and your sack is about to rip open."

"But you said you were proud of me."

"I am, Asgeir," he said, "but I don't want you to be troubled. I must say, I regret not being quieter – but I do wonder if Rudolf ever intended for me to be lawman."

"Why me, then?"

"You're easier to control – younger, a puppy compared to this old dog."

"I am not, Father," Asgeir said. "Haakon caught me in a moment of weakness, but I have braved the storm, I have fought on land and at sea."

"The serpent of the world has yet to wrap you," he said. "All of its weight. It makes bravery into cowardice, many honorable deeds to dishonorable, and good men into evil men. We must be like Thor," he said, and performed a fishing motion. "We must fish up the serpent. We can never defeat it, but just to see its strength wane for but an eyeblink, for it to baulk at our might, that is how we stand true."

"I don't want to hang her," Asgeir said. He thought back to her friendship, and her kiss, back on the beach. "Tormod deserved his death."

"But Orkney didn't," Hallgeir said. "Orkney deserves law, or they have the scepter of Harold Finehair."

"I will try, Father."

"And neither Rudolf nor Haakon are the only ones playing hnefatafl, my son. I too will be three steps ahead of them. I promise you that."

"So I am the lawspeaker of Orkney. I will judge both Fina, as a murderer, and Tormod, as a reaver and rapist, even though he is dead. I will pray to Tyr that I speak the laws well, and I hope that you see my choices as right."

"And we keep Rudolf at range," Hallgeir said. "But yes, son. We're in this together, and by Thor, we will outlive the lot of them, and be mirthful."

Hallgeir embraced his son.

The rains ceased and the sun burned bright in the early spring each day. A platform had been raised where Fina knelt chained up to a post, bundled in a blanket. Eirik slept by her side.

"Eirik," Asgeir said as he approached them, just after first light.

A flutter of his eyelashes, but he failed to stir. Could he hang Fina in the name of freedom for Orkney? Eirik lay there, and then with a low voice, sang a verse from the Sayings of the High One:

To a false friend the footpath winds

Though his house be on the highway.

Fina stuck her tongue out at him after the final lyric.

Asgeir, bereft of words for either, left them. *He thinks me a false friend, but I must behave honorably as lawspeaker.*

Hallgeir's meaty finger pinched the white antler-tine king-piece on the hnefatafl board. With a roll of the sheep-knuckles, Rudolf hemmed in the king with his glass foot-soldiers. Godifu and Rudolf's wife fluted with two leg-bones behind near the hearth-fire of the mead-hall, seated upon the bench.

Asgeir had watched them play the game for two days, and each bout, Rudolf had trumped his father, though Hallgeir never surrendered without the stubbornness of a sea-captain on the deck of his doomed ship. *Ulf.*

A pat on the back drew him from the game, and Eirik stood there with a pair of swords in scabbards. He gestured to leave the hall, and Asgeir found him in his fighting stance.

"We are free men, Asgeir. Free men wield swords and know warcraft. Let us spar."

They sword-danced in the sunset, in the pasture at the edge of the furthest longhouse on the islet. Puffins wheeled overhead as Asgeir and Eirik locked blades, parried, thwarted, and bobbed out of each other's strikes. *I wish I could tell you that I want to spare Fina.*

Hallgeir arrived, and the dour look across his grizzled face told Asgeir who had won the Hnefatafl game. With a wave of his arms, his father parted the two sword-dancers.

"Let me show you lads the skills of Lothlend," he said. "The Nordmenn say we fight like the Irish, and the Irish say we fight like the Nordmenn. No matter – few could best a Lothlend warrior in a duel."

Hallgeir unsheathed his sword and stood in stance with his legs spread. "The weight in your legs. Your feet, first line of defense. Your sword, second. Your shield, third. Master that and you master the duel."

With a lurch, the Housecarl of Lothlend lunged forward. Asgeir faced him and jumped forth, but Hallgeir snapped back, out of the way of Asgeir's sword. Eirik faced Hallgeir, his sword drawn. He mirrored the Gael-Slayer's stance.

Eirik, you fight well. Helvete, Rudolf, this shouldn't be my choice, but now I am lawspeaker.

On the third morning, Rudolf summoned Asgeir to his hall. There, his Svears stood at the ready, armed with their spears and in their yellow coats. Rudolf's mistress stood at his side. Asgeir went with his father, and some of the men from Toke's farm, who had all but abandoned Eirik and his murderous sister.

In front of the longhearth, Rudolf had laid out a chest closed by an iron padlock. He handed Asgeir a whalebone key. He unlocked the chest and there found a brass-buttoned yellow coat folded in the middle. Beneath, he found madder-tinged baggy trousers just like the Svears wore. Under them, a tall salmon-colored hat, capped in a brass cone. Rudolf presented him a shield, yellow-faced.

I'm to dress like a Svear, with this pointed hat and coat?

He looked back at his father, dressed like a Gael from Ireland. His father returned his look with a warm smile and a nod.

Asgeir dressed himself in the loose pants and found two small brass falcon-shaped hooks for his winnigas. *A symbol of Freya. It must be a sign. I must dress as a Svear.*

After he clad himself in the buttoned coat and stood there, a Nordmann-Gael among the Svears, his father handed him Gael-Kisser in its scabbard.

"All in the isles know the sword Gael-Kisser, for its blade was first to fell an Irish king. It was my great-grandfather's. Now you are belted with it."

Asgeir belted himself with the sword, and Godifu handed him a madder-dyed cloak. She broached it under his arm, and Asgeir found it flew in the shape of a weathervane.

The men all filed outside the hall toward the center of the longhouses. Asgeir followed them, all wordless, save for a lyre-player that seemed to strum with each footstep.

Fina walked out. Her hands swung freely at her waist, and her long, black hair was untangled, washed and oily. She wore a simple brown dress with a shawl cinched by a bone-pin at her shoulder. Oddly to Asgeir, she held a long white rod. Eirik walked with her, dressed similarly.

Asgeir stood just nine paces from them. Eirik mouthed *Have pity on her.* Rudolf and his men formed a half-ring around them. Fina seemed to stare not at Asgeir, but through him.

"Fina Frizzy-Hair," Asgeir said after clearing his throat. "You are accused of murdering Tormod Harvaardsson the Colorless."

"End this farce!" she yelled out. "The rapist of Drusticca met a gruesome end – oh, how sad! No one will shed a tear over that slaughtered swine!"

A ripple of gasps and whispers went through the crowd. Men muttered while an old woman fingered a cross pendant around her neck.

Asgeir opened his mouth to speak, but Fina's shriek drowned him out.

"You debased a Christian girl named Drusticca – naked upon the land, dirty, rotten – but your Goddess arrived in my dream!" She held up the long white stick overhead – a whalebone distaff. "A Christian I am no longer, for I die a worshipper of Freya," Fina said, "who has a message for you all! As the distaff weaves yarn, I weave war! Death will be over Orkney! Hang me and I will unleash a sundering of blood and flame! Freya shall spare you all only if you release me unscathed! Fear this grim mask!"

Her face warped in twitches, and with a roll of her shoulders, she twirled the distaff. Much muttering moved throughout the crowd. Before Asgeir could think of a retort, Rudolf grasped him by the arm.

"The blood will flow like waves – yes – I am the prophetess of Freya – she speaks through me!" Fina cried out.

I was going to only outlaw her – but what can I do now, with this horrible speech?

"You must hang her," Hallgeir said to him in a too-loud undertone. "You cannot let her live. Her weirdness will rouse them to arms against us."

"Fina, I demand you end this nonsense at once," Asgeir said.

"The distaff of Freya grants me her power – yes – the man to hang me will find himself in a loveless marriage!"

"Fina, take back what you said – and we may spare you!"

Both Rudolf and Hallgeir growled something in each of his ears but he paid them no mind.

"The so-called Jarl that oversees my hanging shall have his manhood wither."

"Asgeir!" both Hallgeir and Rudolf whispered to him at once.

You've given me no choice, Fina. I am so sorry, and to you too, Eirik. And Drusticca.

"As lawspeaker," Asgeir said so loud that his voice cracked. "Fina has admitted her murder – and she must pay the price."

"You all will pay the price."

"I sentence you to the gallows!"

Many in the crowd gasped. Eirik's mouth dropped open. Fina's eyes widened but she laughed.

"The end of all who befriend you! Freya says my afterwalker shall stalk your every step, Asgeir!"

No, Fina, not like this. I don't want your afterwalker. I want your spirit to rest. I didn't want this burden, and you've made it heavier.

"Gag her," Rudolf said to his men, and they set forth. "Farewell, my brother, Feidelm! Farewell Asgeir, good watchman! Farewell, dreadful Orkney! But banes over a man who touches the apostle of Freya!" she said.

She drew away from a gaggle of men, but one apprehended her, and another wrapped a hemp scrap around her mouth. She chewed at it and rolled her eyes into the back of her head as another ripped the distaff from her and chucked it aside.

Fina, you complete and utter fool. Now I have to live with hanging you.

A crossbeam blemished the meadowy grass outside the longhouses. A noose fluttered in the light breeze. Fina writhed her shoulders and chewed at her gag and clawed at the hangmen until they tied her hands behind her back. When they led her to a stool, she kicked it over, and then with a twist of her lithe form and a knee to the groin, a hangman doubled over with a groan. He staggered up, they tied her feet together and put her neck into the noose. Rudolf stepped forward with a loudhailer, downwind in the balmy air.

"Today we mark the death of a doer of a misdeed. May her death be in the name of Odin, so that he may avert the wars she promises come this way. In the name of the Allfather, the hangman, the Lord of the Gallows – to your death, criminal wretch."

With his heel, Rudolf toppled the stool. The noose tightened around her neck as her bound feet swung about. Asgeir turned to look away, but to his surprise, Eirik tugged on his hair and pointed toward her. He said nothing, but the flicker in his eyes ensured Asgeir would watch.

Fina hung lifeless there on the sward. Some sheep bleated in the distance. Eirik released Asgeir's hair as a falcon flew over the herd, but grasped his head again and motioned it back to the dangling body of his sister.

This is no fault of mine. Blame Tormod for plunder and rape. Blame Jarl Toke for vanishing. Blame Fina for her ceaseless rant. Blame anyone but me, for this is not upon me.

Is it? I am the lawspeaker. Maybe I could have stopped this, as I could have stopped Tormod.

Rudolf cleared his throat as he stood in front of the blued Fina while she stilled. His lyre-player strummed a note. Rudolf sang:

In green Uppsala's hills,
Bedecked in the criminals killed.
All-Father guides our hand,
From the vagrant to cleanse the land.

The lyre echoed each word, and when he finished, Rudolf righted the stool and stood on it as a dais.

"See that neither farmer nor slave will be spared Odin's death. Unlike your so-called Jarl Toke, I will not tolerate the vagrant, the criminal, the bandit, in my land. Tormod too deserved this death – but by the lash of the lawman's tongue, not Balder's bane. Furthermore, I am a noble-blooded man myself, and it is also an affront to Odin that a thrall has murdered a nobleman, criminal or not. Therefore, I charge his estate with allowing such vagrancy and for keeping poor watch over their thralls, and raising such a vicious wench. What say you, lawspeaker?"

"Salt in the wound," Eirik said. "Her soul is hardly in Hel!"

"Hold your tongue, Eirik of Toke," Rudolf said. "Lawspeaker – whose farm was this murderous thrall-girl from?"

"The holding of Jarl Toke on Rousay."

"Should we be surprised?" Rudolf asked the crowd. "Jarl Toke's own hatchling, perhaps. I suggest, lawspeaker, that you vacant the Jarl's claim over his land."

"I'll give it back to you," Asgeir whispered to Eirik.

"I don't want a farm, I want my sisters back, Asgeir," he said.

Hallgeir had leaned in to listen.

"No, Asgeir," Hallgeir said to him in an undertone. "Not after that display of Fina's. He may take revenge."

"Then I shall take it for my own," Asgeir said in a moment of brightness, "for I have worked there and know it well, and I will keep Eirik under my thumb." He spoke to the crowd. "I, Asgeir Hallgeirsson, lawspeaker of Rudolf High-Hat, declare that I am the owner of Jarl Toke's farm."

Eirik just stared back at him, fish-mouthed, wide-eyed. "Salt in the wounds," he muttered.

"Smart," Hallgeir whispered to his son. "Always three steps ahead."

"Then so be it – Asgeir has taken the estate of Jarl Toke, and his thralls along with it. Asgeir, you know you will be responsible for the discipline of Toke's thralls, as they are now yours. I suggest the whip." Rudolf now addressed the crowd. "Today, we shall venture forth across Orkney, and gather many farmers. I shall ask for your wapentake for Jarl – and by the Gods, if you say yes, I will lead Orkney against the feeders of eagle."

Rudolf then spoke of his noble bloodline, to the Ynglings and to Freyr himself, and he spoke long and well of his deeds in Svearia, on Gotland, of his raids in Curland, and so forth, but Asgeir found the words hadn't reached his ears. He just stared at the rocking body of Fina.

Eirik had left. Asgeir's cloak had come undone, and he fumbled with both ends of it along with the weathervane pin before the wind could take it. When he looked up, he spotted a tall flag flying over the rocky stretch of Birsay.

Many in the crowd gasped as Rudolf stopped midsentence to turn and look. A weathervane, scarlet, traveled downwind sunwise around Birsay.

The crowd gathered along the cliffside to witness the warship there. Many spearmen stood from bow to stern, and when Asgeir reached the edge of the cliff, a collective gasp sounded when a second ship rounded the islet, and then a third, all as long and crammed with armed men as the first.

"Vikings!" an old woman shouted. With a rush, the crowd vanished as they fled for the houses and further afield across the island to hide from the coming storm.

"My sister's prophecy was right," Eirik said with a laugh as he prodded Asgeir. "Enjoy the din of spears, lawspeaker."

"Men, at arms," Rudolf said to his men, and Asgeir knew it included him.

"They look like Nordmenn's ships – with those prowfigures. I fight at your side, son," Hallgeir said. "Listen to me, and we will survive."

"I have sworn no oath to him – but I wear his men's clothes. I am his lawspeaker. Honor demands I fight. Now I will regain it."

The men followed the ships as they rounded the island and arrived at the landing place. All three dropped anchor. In the first ship with the brightest red weathervane, sailors lowered a small boat down. Two rowers heaved a standing man across the short span toward the stairs leading up to Birsay.

Rudolf High-Hat stood at the ledge of the wooden staircase surrounded by his men. When Asgeir reached them, he knew the man in the boat, one foot on the prow, sworded, red-cloaked. *Jarl Haakon!*

"And we worried the Gods lost our favor – my enemy shows up at my doorstep," Rudolf said to his men. "Jarl Haakon of Borgund," he yelled down at the boat as it drifted in the lowering tide.

"Rudolf High-Hat," Haakon said. "No surprise that it's you here when I sought to find raiders. Now listen to what I say, by orders of the King."

"I care not who orders you. You killed my son without trial."

"To Odin with the vagrant, the criminal."

"'To Helvete with law' is what you had said," Rudolf said. "Then know that your nephew, Tormod Harvaardsson, a viking – and worse, a rapist – has too been killed unjustly."

"My nephew? Dead? How dare you – and where is his body?" Haakon said as he bit his lip.

"I will not trade words with you for it – for I know not where Arild Rudolfsson's headless body is – so save your breath."

"To hear such a misdeed – I am no longer here to parley, Rudolf. You shouted to all Nordmenn that you are a lawless viking, a flea upon a bite-ridden Orkney. I have come to settle these raids by law, and outlaw your snake of a wife, Frida Half-Plait, to Iceland."

"What did you dare call my wife?"

Asgeir raised an eyebrow. *He has called her much worse – but what man would insult another's wife?*

"The Jarl Toke has been lost to Ran, and I have come here, by decree of Harald, to establish the Jarldom of Orkney in his stead."

"Harald's puppy," Rudolf said with a spit.

"You dare spit in his name?"

"I do, for we men of Orkney bow to no one," Rudolf said and spat down the cliff. He turned to the men behind him. "You see? Jarl Toke dies – and now Harald believes he has the right to chain us. I, for one, say no."

The men all shouted back: *No!*

"I knew you hadn't the sense to be reasoned with," Haakon said. "I have three drakkar here, and you can count my oarsmen. Further, I have already claimed Toke's estate. Many of the freemen have sworn loyalty just in the few hours after our arrival. Rudolf, surrender Birsay to me, and you and your men will be spared."

"Surrender to me, and perhaps after you are dead, men will not snicker about Harald's little puppydog."

"You'll die like your son did – on his knees, begging like a whore."

Rudolf unsheathed his sword and poised it at Haakon.

Harald's Jarl was rowed back to his ship as Rudolf turned to his men.

"To arms – all of you. We defend Birsay. We have higher ground – they must walk uphill to us. We have an advantage – use it."

A stamp of men trotted around Birsay. Spears, axes, bows, javelins, swords, shields. Rudolf and his vanguard of housecarls all lined up at the forefront, Asgeir among them. Rudolf himself handed him a spear and a shield painted white and red and edged in brass – the shield of Rudolf. Hallgeir had his spear and shield behind his son.

"As I said, son – I will fight alongside you. And you will live."

Below at the stand, when the tide edged away, the army edged in. Rows of spearmen in a wall waited there in the wet sand. The foremost of them wore red cloaks, scarlet like the weathervane, and their brass brooches glinted in the sun. They waited at the command of Haakon, who brushed his long blond hair with a comb. *They must outnumber us nine to one.*

"I understand, Father."

"My sister always said the Gods loved you. You're lucky."

Once Haakon's sailors rowed him back toward his fleet, he unhooked a horn from his neck and blew into it. A long *moo.* With a shout and a wave of his hand, countless sailors clambered down the rails of their anchored ships. A horde of spearmen waded through the waist-deep water in a great slosh, so much that the tide seemed to rise higher from so many bodies.

Upon Birsay, tens of warriors came forth armed – spears and axes and a great match of shields. Asgeir scanned the crowd and found the men from the battle at Toke's farm. They looked forlorn there, weaponless and leaderless.

"Men," Rudolf said to them as he approached. "The Norns have woven our fate, and we are here. Jarl Haakon will not spare us if he wins – if not by sword, then by chain. Let us fight for our gracious host. To arms, men!"

The eight men shouted and scrambled to find weapon and shield with the rest. Beyond them, Asgeir found Eirik seated on the stool next to his hanged sister.

"Eirik, we fight."

"What did you say?" he asked without looking up.

"I said we must fight. Don't you remember I fought against Tormod for you? And your sisters, they were my friends, just as you are, and we chased after him so we may rescue Drusticca."

"I meant that I didn't understand you, since you were not speaking the Normann's tongue, but the Svear's."

"Remember what you told me, Eirik, after you attempted to work me as a thrall, and that whoreson Earp had walloped me, dragged me in cowmuck, and whipped me like a dog? 'Don't whine at your fate. Reject your lament. Hold fast against dread.'"

Eirik's eyes widened and his neck stiffened, but the clamor of battle raged at the edge of Birsay.

"Be careful, my friend. I fight under the eye of the God of Spears. I suggest you hide yourself, if you have no heart for the fight," Asgeir said.

A pair of crows flew overhead as he left the gallows. A few of the warriors broke from the cluster, gaping up at the cawing signs from the All-Father of War. *Did Fina really speak as Freya's volva?*

Rudolf stood at the entrance of the longhouse of Birsay. He held a two-handed spear in his hands with a long yellow banner waving from its spearhead. "They may outnumber us, but we shall not let them up here. Block the entrance – largest shields forward!"

Asgeir found that his shield ran from chin to knee, his spear set behind it, with Gael-Kisser at his side if his spear broke or the lines vanished and the battle delved down to duels. As he paced across the sward with his men, he glanced over and found several warriors grouped together broken off from Rudolf's eager men. They huddled there, armed with spears, shielded, as if they awaited a command.

"Son, that looks odd," Hallgeir said, himself armed with a shield so big it was door-like.

"They haven't responded to Rudolf? What are they doing? Maybe they're unconvinced of Rudolf's zest, and they see we are outnumbered, high position though we may have. They may waylay us, so must keep watch on them."

Rudolf shouted at a group of javelin-armed men who cast them down from the cliffside. Another trio of men nocked arrows and aimed their bows. *Reckless, Haakon. You'll never take the fort. Is this the price of honor? No, the wrath of Thor has him.*

A storm of men, like a torrent of tramping beasts, whirled up the staircase. The thuds of iron against wood sounded the clash of the two warbands, Rudolf and Haakon behind them, urging both lines forward so that one side might take the stronghold.

The must of sweat mixed with brine harrowed over the fort. Rows of men waited, among the longhouses, shoving forward in a mass to fight on the staircase. The javelin-casters and bowmen loosened their darts from the edge, until a bowman yelled, crashed backward and slid from the cliffside with a javelin through his leg. The ranged attackers backed off as the staircase itself trembled, its boards and nails all loosened from too much weight and movement and hits from weapons.

Shields flung down below to the ebbing tides and the strand was now wet with blood. Men lay crumbled under their shields like crushed beetles. One of Rudolf's men lost his shield and it rolled down, tripped an enemy, and three of them tumbled. The din of iron, wood, screams, slashes, stabs, all threatened to loosen the staircase from the cliffside.

"Asgeir!" Hallgeir shouted at him, and the lad understood it was not the first time his father yelled his name.

Eighteen freemen stood spear-armed among the longhouses.

"Rudolf High-Hat," shouted Audun, armed now with a longspear. They hadn't caught his attention, as he had been near the frontline. They beat their spearshafts against their shields.

"Asgeir, I was right! Audun and his men fight for Haakon – beware," Hallgeir said.

Rudolf, now hatless, turned toward them with a puzzled look.

"Lay down your arms – in the name of King Harald," Audun said.

Rudolf shouted something unheard, for the clangs of battle had grown too high.

"Forward, men!" Audun shouted.

Hallgeir raised his spear upward. "Form a line!"

Asgeir gathered up with many of Rudolf's men, but they were outnumbered threefold. An iron-tip darted at Asgeir's face. He raised his shield and ducked behind it – it flew overhead and clanked across a short wall.

"Odin owns you all!" Audun shouted as they charged.

The longspear thrust forward. Hallgeir jumped out of the way as the enemy flank threatened to swallow them.

"We need help!"

"Help – traitors – enemies up here!" Asgeir shouted as more of Rudolf's men broke off and joined the foemen.

There on the paved ground between the longhouses, Asgeir's spear vied for his enemies. Spears thudded against shieldfaces like drumbeats. The man on his right side hobbled out of the line as he held his own guts in his belly, and now Asgeir found himself against three. He leapt over a ruined stone wall and held his shield to cover his torso. Three spears struck for him, grazing the rawhide edge of his shield, batting against the blocks of the wall, and into the turf-walled house behind him.

When one enemy leapt over, he pivoted and struck him in the side with his spear. He ripped the spear out as the man tumbled down and never got up, but the two others leapt. With a cry, Asgeir turned to find Hallgeir behind them.

Hallgeir's spear crashed through an enemy's jaw. The third foemen, between the two, cast his weapons down and himself on his knees. Asgeir and his father rejoined the line, and as Hallgeir turned the corner, more enemies came out from the house.

"To fight alongside my father – an honor. I will do you proud, Pappa."

One struck a spear at Asgeir who parried with his own shaft. A screaming foursome of girls ran out the rear gangway as Asgeir charged into the house with his shield forward. Hallgeir charged in after the girls ran out, shield-first, knocking over one foeman while the other two fled, as if they faced a loose bull. Asgeir slammed the rim of his shield into the shin of one enemy and when he retched, stabbed him in the thigh. That man slipped on an upturned rug, dipped and tramped through a still-blazing longfire. He cried out as he kicked up coals and embers and rolled about the floor.

"More in the bathhouse! Come!" Hallgeir yelled and went out the same way he came in, and Asgeir followed.

They raced around a small house and into the smokeless bathhouse. An enemy met them just behind the ingang. It was Audun, his sword wet and his eyes like a berserkerganger. He bit the rim of his shield as he rushed Hallgeir, his spearshaft held down by his shield. Hallgeir blocked and Audun crashed into it, the two dueling their shields while Audun raised his sword to slash Asgeir's father.

Asgeir dropped his spear and tried to unsheathe his sword. It would not budge out of its fleeced sheath. "Helvete!"

All three leather straps tugged at the baldric of Gael-Kisser. Asgeir squeezed and pried and shimmied but the bane of Gaelic kings stayed put. Hallgeir shoved forward with a bear-like yell, but Audun sidestepped and let Hallgeir crash face-first into the stone bench.

"Father!"

Audun stayed his sword from Hallgeir when he caught sight of Asgeir.

"You humiliated me – now I will slay you before your father – traitors! I serve the rightful man, not a Svear usurper!"

Audun raised his sword as he came within striking range of Asgeir, who scrapped for his spearshaft.

"Til Valhal!" a fourth voice cried.

With a thud, someone tackled Audun. His father had regained his footing, but it was not him. Asgeir saw a shirtless Eirik upon Audun, wrestling for the sword-arm.

Audun lifted his shield to bash Eirik, spittle flying free, but Hallgeir stabbed him through the chest with a spear. He groaned and his eyes went lightless.

"More enemies about," Hallgeir said and wiped the blood from his nose. "Out now."

"Father, you're unwounded?"

"I fare well – takes more than that!"

"Thank you, Eirik, thank you!" Asgeir said.

"I couldn't just let my friend die," Eirik said. "You were a good watchman when Tormod came. I know you did your duty as lawspeaker, Asgeir."

"Asgeir – now!" Hallgeir yelled.

As Eirik crawled out from under the lifeless Audun, Asgeir raced outside.

Haakon's men had advanced. Now the fight reached the sward. A row of men fought, two abreast on the staircase against three or four. The wounded and dead lay around, twixt the longhouses, slumped over walls, clustered around the ruined church, further up in the meadows. At the staircase, men waited their turn to fight, since the crammed space of death left no room for others.

"Hold!" Rudolf shouted. "Hold!" he shouted again, and again, as if he shouted after each draw of breath.

The staircase creaked. It cracked. The highest-climbed man of Haakon parted his lips to yell. The staircase wobbled one way, and another, as the handrail snapped off and the structure lost its footing. It swayed and knocked men off it like hapless riders on a wild-bucking horse, and then upturned with a waterfall of men to plummet down below. The foremost warrior slipped on a pool of blood and vanished along with the lot of them. Rudolf's men were silenced for a long while, save for some moans of wounded, with nothing but the gentle droplets of rain to Asgeir's ears.

"Odin favors us!" Rudolf said. "The fight is not over yet – onward – may no enemy survive!"

Asgeir walked toward the cliffside. Down below, a wreckage of men and wood and weapons all littered the now tideless strand. He climbed down the bloodied cliffside, across outcrops where a stray finger lay. Two of the ships had already left, but the third seacraft, the closest to the shoreline, had slumped over without water underneath it. Many of Haakon's sailors stood on the foreshore. Some of them raced toward the other side, to the mainland, climbed up and fled. Haakon himself, with a shredded cloak, reached a deck. Other men, caught on land, cast down their weapons and fell to their knees.

"Draw no quarter, blood must spill for Arild Rudolfsson," Rudolf said, and his men marched forward to stab the surrendered enemies, one by one.

Rudolf's men shouted and cheered and others poked and prodded about the corpses to snatch silver rings or brass brooches. Rudolf held up a hand.

"Stop!" he shouted. "We have not won yet – Haakon has escaped! The battle is still on – men, unbeach this ship!"

With ropes and tether, Rudolf's warriors pulled the ship into the sea, Asgeir among them. When they climbed into the ship, they found one survivor there from Haakon.

Rudolf had his men bring him before them. He was a young man with a swollen face, no older than thirteen winters. Rudolf touched his sword to the youth's neck.

"Haakon said farmers have pledged loyalty to him – who and where are they?"

"At Evie, Westray, Edday, Egilsay..."

"And he has his estate on Rousay?"

"Yes – please, don't kill me!"

With a hack, the youth lost his head. It rolled over the deck of the ship, and Rudolf's men gasped at that.

"I have no patience for cowardly pleas – rid us of this rubbish. Set sail!"

Rudolf leaned over and picked up the headless body, pressed it against the gunwale, and flipped it off the ship, smearing his coat in blood. "I will have your wives wash this out," he said to his sailors as he shook the blood from his hands. He peaked his head over the rail to the men down below. "Board the ship." He turned to his men. "Rowers – course for Evie! Afterward we take the islands one by one, and tonight, the head of Haakon garnishes Toke's farm."

The sail unfurled and Asgeir sat on an unknown man's locked chest, and rowed the ship southward along the coast.

Jarl Haakon – you did me wrong. I fear that this Rudolf will be no better, but I come for you. Now I shall have my honor that you stole from me. Now I shall show my father that I deserve to war alongside him.

CHAPTER VIII

Thor's Wrath

The nameless ship stormed along the coast in search of unruly farmers. With each dock, the sailors hit the shore, their oars traded for spears and axes and swords. With each stroke of the oars, another farmhouse burnt. The smoke, the ash, the screams. With each push to sea, one more head-on-stake adorned the farm's landing place. By late afternoon, the keel dipped deeper, weighted by plunder.

Rudolf stood near the boom while he gestured the men toward Rousay, to Jarl Toke's farm. They coursed there, where Haakon's other two ships had beached.

Hallgeir rose from his seat and spoke to Rudolf.

"You've forced us to go a'viking, this was what Haakon feared."

"Then let him fear," Rudolf said. He rested his sword on his right shoulder.

"Whatever comes of this day, Harald will hear of it."

"And he will tremble."

Asgeir found the two of them athwart the other. Hallgeir's spear sheened in the sun, while Rudolf righted his own hat in the wind.

"We pay for this with our blood," Hallgeir said and left him.

"My sword will not sheath until it drinks the blood of Haakon," Rudolf said to Hallgeir's back.

Hallgeir sat on the chest behind Asgeir.

"I don't like this, son. That Pictish girl shrieked of war, like Gullinkambi, the cock who heralds Ragnarok. And this all isn't our fight."

"It's about my honor, father. I must fight."

Hallgeir ran a hand through his sharp beard. "And who taught you that – Rudolf High-Hat? That is not honor, son. It's not senseless fighting, no matter how brave your heart, skilled your hand, or true your strikes. Honor in the fight is the right deed, against a baleful opponent, bravery in the face of someone more powerful than you. Have you not heard the sayings of the High One? It is Odin, our forebear, I quote: 'If a man is wicked, then say so'."

Asgeir halted the stroke of his oar, and for an eyeblink, went thoughtless.

His father frowned and gazed off toward the horizon.

Rudolf held aloft his sword as many foemen mustered at the headland of Toke's farm. They stood near the mounds twixt the wooden gravemarkers. "Ready, bowmen…"

A *thwap*. Rudolf gazed at his own hand. An arrow stuck through the meat under his thumb, mid-shaft. The goosefeathers ruffled in the breeze as he unslung his shield with his good hand, and with a scowl, kneeled behind it.

"Shields!" Hallgeir yelled at Asgeir. They unfastened the shields from the gunwale and hid behind them as more arrows rained upon the ship, clattering about the deck like a box of loose nails.

The tide threatened to catch the ship, but she slid broadside, and crashed headlong into the shore. The keel skidded and rammed through the ground and pierced a mound, tearing it and the skeleton asunder in its green grave. Asgeir was flung forward and landed gracelessly between two chests. He climbed to his feet as pain seeped up his hip, but the battle raged again. *Father war.*

The sailors leapt from the gunwales, shields first, as the remnant of Haakon's force met them in combat. From among the farmstead, a woman crowed, and the she-thralls, known by their undyed clothes, scattered among the buildings. A sheepdog fled uphill as the men tramped over uncut grass.

Nearby, by a boathouse, a girl hasted away. When she dropped her bucket and flounders spilled out, her brown hood flopped back off her head, and Asgeir spotted her face. She had dark eyes, pale skin, and from her height and hips, he knew her, and she fled uphill with the rest of them.

"Sakka!" he said, as he climbed over the gunwale. "Sakka, you're here!" A horn trumpeted from the farmstead as the tramp of Haakon's men passed. "I'll survive this, Sakka, just so I may be with you again."

Rudolf kept pace with his guard, arrow still through his hand. At the end of the headland, Haakon led his men, shields raised, spears forward.

Asgeir caught sight of Haakon, his red cloak aflutter behind him. He remembered then, Arild on his hands and knees, begging, pleading, and Haakon hectoring him to slay him unlawfully. *What have you done to me, you bastard? You come here to claim law, yet you unjustly killed Arild? I'll see your death.*

Both sides stopped just a span from the other.

"Cast!"

"Cast!"

The javelins hurled through the air. They cracked through shields, and a man at Asgeir's flank crumpled in a hiss of breath.

"Forward!"

"Forward!"

Both lines of men filled the headland from left to right. Asgeir knew not which side had more men. He hadn't the slightest, for he found no men to count, just enemies. Thor, in his wrath by the whetstone lodged in his forehead, reddened Asgeir as red as his beard. The sound of a lyre winked from behind the enemy line, and Asgeir knew not if it was real or some kind of God's song.

Hesitance overcame them as the shieldwalls formed. The haste of battle faded to the hazards of the sharp iron rods that glinted in the sun. The urge of Haakon and Rudolf, the tramp of their feet, the drum of spearshaft against shieldface tranced them and they edged closer. Just as the longest spears threatened to tap, someone burst onto the battlefield.

"By Freya and Freyr you will halt!" a woman's voice cried. Flying from one flank to the other, she grabbed ahold of spearshafts, kicked away javelins, slapped away axes on both battlelines. On the furthest flank to the west, the rhythm of spears embarked, but on the eastern flank and in the center, a bewilderment spread, until all men ceased fighting. "I demand you halt! By the twins of peace, you will not begin this slaughter!"

The red of Asgeir's vision lessened. He found her there, Saga the Healer, wife of Haakon, ankle-deep in mud on the headland. Her red ankle-length dress contrasted against the war-tunics of the fighters, her linen wimple fluttered behind her, the thick plait of her blond hair rigid against her breast. The two oval-shaped brass brooches that held her over-dress glowed in the sunlight. She stepped on a low mound, losing one shoe to the suck of the soggy ground. She kicked off her other shoe, snatched it off the ground and then slammed it back down.

"In my twenty-six winters, I have never seen such slaughter. I haven't the time to fix the wounds. There's too much gore! Blood! Ashes! Death! I demand you halt all this!"

Haakon stepped forward through his own men.

"Saga, get off the battlefield – you could have been killed!"

"And so what? How many have already died because of you?"

"Because of him." Haakon pointed toward Rudolf.

"I'll have your head for what you did to my son," Rudolf said.

"I'll have yours, Rudolf. Saga, step away."

With a snarl, Saga tore off her brass oval brooches from her breasts to let her apron-dress fall down. She stood there, in a soiled linen underdress, with her arms outstretched as she grabbed ahold of her hair with both of her hands.

"If you refuse to make peace, then our marriage shall split!"

Haakon said nothing, but his mouth wrung. Asgeir caught Rudolf smirking, the only time he had ever seen him do so.

"I agree with Haakon," Rudolf said. "The battlefield is no place for a woman. Move out of the way."

"I will not," she said, and paced to and fro. "I will not! I will stand in front of your spears, I will throw myself on your shields, I will stick my head out for your axes!"

"War surprises you? You've been my wife for over ten years. You travelled with us, down to the lands of Danes and Wends and Franks."

"I will not see this senseless slaughter! Haakon – Rudolf – settle it in a duel, and stop the death of so many of our kinsmen!"

Haakon and Rudolf approached each other in the center of their men. Saga stood there, tugging at her now unbraided hair.

"You slew my son, Haakon," Rudolf said.

"He was a viking," Haakon said and pointed at him. "As are you."

"You slew him like an oathbreaker, without trial."

"He deserved none."

Rudolf shifted the sword over his shoulder. "All deserve trial, Haakon."

"And my nephew did not?" Haakon clenched his fist over the pommel of his sword.

"That was not I. Your nephew was a viking, and the Gods punished him for it. But he was murdered, himself, by the sister of a Pictish thrall he raped."

"And where is that murderer?"

"The lawspeaker sentenced her to hang," Rudolf said.

Asgeir ran his finger along the brass buttons of his coat, as if to rip it off.

"And how do I know this is truthful?" Haakon asked.

"There are many witnesses. Even the murderer's brother," Rudolf said, shifting his sword again.

"An array of wrongs," Haakon said, "and a misjudgment of the law by your lawspeaker. That is why you shall all submit to Harald."

"We of Orkney will never submit to a king," Rudolf said. "Not will – shall. Kill me, and Harald will send three more Jarls with nine more fleets before summer's end."

"Let this end with a duel then, Haakon. Tyr decides who is right and wrong, in the duel circle."

"Rudolf, I agree with you, and Saga. Let us spare our men, this must end with a duel."

Rudolf held up his arrow-pierced hand. "A duel would bring glory to the Gods, but my sword-arm is damaged."

"Bring me the lawspeaker, then," Haakon said, "who robbed me of justice for my son's killer."

Asgeir looked up at his father. His father met his stare. "I knew he thought three steps ahead, but let me, son."

"No, father. Honor calls me. I must do the right deed, and say that this man is wicked. Then maybe I'd be welcomed to Valhal."

"I knew you'd come to your senses, and I know there's nothing I can say to off-set your course. Just make me proud, by remembering your training. You are lucky, and by Thor, I will not outlive you."

"So be it – he will fight in my stead, to avenge Arild's unjust death," Rudolf said. "Come forth, lawspeaker."

Asgeir walked forward, thoughtless, his sword still sheathed.

"The son of the Gael-Slayer? Asgeir?"

"Yes, Haakon. A man who witnessed your misdeed will bring my son justice."

Haakon unsheathed his sword. "I heard you drowned along with that bastard, Ulf. Even then, forethought you to die by that spear wound. I finally see ill-luck is upon you, for this duel is to the death."

Both lines of men ringed around the two duelists.

"Asgeir, son of Hallgeir, lawspeaker of Rudolf, shall fight in my stead. If he wins, Jarl Haakon's men shall return to Norway, and tell Harald that the Jarldom is under the command of Rudolf High-Hat."

"I, Jarl Haakon of Borgund, shall fight. If I win, then Rudolf High-Hat and all his supporters end their claim over Orkney, and shall be banished from all Harald's Isles, outlawed to Iceland."

"It is settled."

"I agree." Rudolf glanced at Asgeir, and pointed his sword at him.

Asgeir cast a glance behind him toward his father as pearls of sweat dripped down his nose. He looked over at Saga, still on the mound, crouched down with a hand over her mouth.

"Footwork, son," Hallgeir shouted over the crowd. "Remember your feet are your first defense, and first offense. Your shield is your second offense Your sword, your second defense, and third offense."

"I'll remember, father," he said. "And what Njall, and Ulf, taught me," he said in an undertone.

"And remember honor – the deeds of each dead man live forevermore."

Haakon stood there, sword unsheathed, shield at-the-ready. *Ullr, you've not come to guide me this time. But I know I can defeat him. I must make my father proud, and not grieve.*

"Unlike Arild, Haakon, I will kill you while you stand."

Asgeir stepped into the dueling ring and there the blades flashed. The gray of Haakon's sword whirled. First it struck for his shoulder and when Asgeir raised his own sword to parry, the Jarl let loose his sword at Asgeir's thigh.

Feet!

Asgeir snapped back like a scared cat.

Feet!

He lunged in at his enemy's flank, a strike at Haakon, who parried with his blade. Asgeir's sword slid up and down Haakon's, their wrists twisted as their weapons hissed. Asgeir stepped forward to jam the sword toward Haakon's face, but the Jarl raised his shield.

Shield!

Asgeir slammed the rim of the shield into Haakon's shield, and bent it back. With a cry, Haakon staggered and lost his footing.

Sword!

Battle-lightning, the streak of swords, cracked. With a slice of Gael-Kisser a chunk of Haakon's shoulder flew off, butchered meat. The men of both Jarls gasped as Haakon's red tunic had been split in twain, his arm rent.

Haakon lost his shield that rolled away, and his sword dropped in a thunk. He held the butchered shoulder, blood flooded through his fingers, and he mouthed a word, "defeat". The Jarl of Borgund crouched, as if to stave off the pain, but slumped to his rear and wheeled on the ground while he bit his bottom lip.

Asgeir watched him down there. Eyeblinks but long ones, longer than he had seen. Haakon's shoulder was nothing but a red haunch. His fingers twitched. His sword slipped from his hand.

A surge of men surrounded them. Rudolf raised his unsheathed sword in his wounded hand to pass to Asgeir. *Tyrfing. The sword that must drink blood before sheathing.*

"The duel was to the death," he said. "Now kill him, with Tyrfing, so it may be sheathed."

"It's not right for me to die so far from home," Haakon said, as he lowered further to the ground.

"You claimed this land as yours," Rudolf said. "So you are home, and at your grave. Asgeir!"

Asgeir looked at Rudolf, his face wrenched. Gael-Kisser hung aloft in his hand. For an eyeblink, he found Arild there, not Haakon. *I can't do this again.*

"He will not survive that," Rudolf said, "so slay him for Odin. You are among the levied of Orkney now, Asgeir, son of Hallgeir, and you do what I say."

"I felled him in the duel – but if you want him dead, then you kill him," Asgeir said, dropped Rudolf's sword, and walked out of the ring. "So says the lawspeaker, Rudolf."

"So I am the hand of death," Rudolf said after a pause.

He seized the sword with his unwounded hand as Haakon met his gaze from the ground.

Asgeir turned and walked through the crowd of warriors as Haakon gurgled after the third whack, and that allowed Rudolf to sheath Tyrfing. He passed Saga, on the mound alone, her eyeshadow in black streaks down her high cheekbones.

After a long stroll along the beach of Toke's farm, he found the kelpy beach where he once walked with Fina. The tide rolled in from the north. His eyes followed it all the way to the headland, where Haakon's men dragged his headless body into a small boat, pushed it out to sea, and rowed away into the grayness of the sound.

In the old Pictish graveyard, he ripped off his Svear-coat; buttons tore through the seams and shattered its stitching. With a wrung of his wrists, the cord of his baggy trousers snapped and they slipped down. Next, his hat tumbled away. His shield sent awhirl into the gray sea. *No, Feidelm, I don't speak like a Svear.*

In his linen undertunic and britches, he seated himself on the upturned, despoiled mound that the ship had pounded. Outsitting, as they called it, when one sleeps upon the dwelling of the dead. He thought of Sakka, and knew he would find her on Rousay, and they would reunite at last. He ought to thank Haakon for that. For a long while, he shut his eyes, and all the sounds vanished save for the lull of the sea. Twixt awake and sleeping, he dreamt for just a spell.

"You must travel away from here," said a manly voice. It awayed from him, distant, as if spoken through a conch shell. "Be afraid not to tell Rudolf the truth, travel from this war-torn land, and I will guide you to safety."

"Thank you, Njordr."

Someone shook him, and he opened his eyes. Eirik stood there, his face spangled in specks of blood.

"Asgeir, what do you do here? We've won the day, there is much joy at Toke's farm."

"I ask for the guidance of our gods."

Eirik sat down next to him. Much noise came from the foreshore and the farmstead. Horses, men, and iron, but Asgeir hadn't turned to look.

"Have you gotten your honor?"

"I think I have, Eirik."

Eirik trudged down the mound, and when his black hair vanished to the scarred graveyard, he came back with something in his hands. A bleached man's skull. It sat in his palm and he spoke to it.

"Alas, my alderelder has spoken to me. I have never forsaken my gods. The White Christ ended their worship, until the flashes of merriment of the Heathen gods pulled me back to them. I understand now, nameless grandfather. I follow the wisdom of the heathen God, Odin. Friendship."

Eirik sang:

Hotter than fire among false hearts burns
Friendship for five days.

Asgeir knew the poem, a verse from the sayings of the High One, the words of Odin himself. He shot to his feet and sang so loud his lungs strained:

But suddenly slackens when the sixth dawns:
Feeble their friendship then.

"You were no feeble friend to me, Asgeir. I do not hate you for Fina's fate. Now, let us go merrymake together at the feast."

The skull grinning from the mound, Asgeir and Eirik left for Toke's former farm to the feast.

CHAPTER IX

The Outlaw

Many men toiled in the fields of Toke's farm. Shirtless, sweaty, downtrodden. Haakon's defeated – his loyalists, of high blood – now thralls waist-deep in the barley field. Midsummer approached as all the men of Orkney awaited the looming news from Norway.

Asgeir stood under the roof of the longhouse, hammer in his hand, nails twixt his teeth. He wore neither yellow kaftan nor pointed, brass-capped hat, but a red cloak he had purchased with Jarl Toke's silver, his portion of the spoils. He nailed the board into the wood until Hallgeir approached, cloaked in his piebald Gael-wrap.

"Your reward has been bountiful, my son. I am happy that we live as free men again."

"No reward would be high enough than freedom. You taught me to never kill a man on his knees. And besides, I was tired of being Rudolf's puppy."

Hallgeir placed a hand on Asgeir's shoulder. "Neither of us are puppies, Asgeir. We are free men, because we're from Odin's loins. Whether it's Rudolf or Haakon or Harald, let the Gods know that we have balls."

At the trackway that led down from the hills, Eirik drove a herd of she-thralls to the farm. The lost property of Haakon, hidden in the moors and old Pictish ruins of the island.

"I worked hard to secure this wife for you, Asgeir. Rudolf is soured by your unwillingness to kill for him, but to Helvete with that. I bargained and I got her for you. She is skilled with the needle, she is beautiful with shapely hips and a soft voice. By Njordr, I hope your mother, sister, and your aunt Bjorg arrive for your wedding."

Asgeir sighed. "Father, you know how I feel about this."

"She's a lofty lady, with a courageous spirit – why, how many women do you know would lope across a battle? And you know firsthand, of her skillful hand."

"I know, father." The spear scar on his chest bristled against his tunic. "But my heart lies elsewhere."

"Your heart can lie with whichever woman behooves it. Asgeir, she is highborn, and has land and powerful relatives back in Sognefjord. That's what marriage is for. Not where the heart lies."

Asgeir hammered the last nail into the board, bent it with a pair of tongs, and nailed it in. *Frigga – you came to me in a dream, you of all wives know who to marry, and now I know who I must marry.*

"I suppose I'll learn to love her."

"Asgeir!" the voice of Eirik cried from meadowland. "Your new thralls have arrived!"

Eirik paced to and fro along the line of she-thralls. Nine of them, girls to women. He pointed up toward the hilly center of the island. One looked pithy and outright mannish, with a face hidden under a thick Pictish hood.

"The escaped thralls. We caught them! They belong to the land, and now the land is ours again, that their master's body lies back in Norway. Maybe that Finngirl you thought you saw is here among them?" He sniffed the stuffy thrall, face sunk into a hood. "But this one smells familiar."

Asgeir climbed down from the roof while Eirik poked the belly of the largest one in line, who squirmed. The thrall let out a chuckle, as if tickled. The hood drew back and Asgeir knew that thrall no woman, but a brawny black-haired shaven-faced man.

"Earp?" Asgeir said with a laugh. He laughed hard, so much his side spasmed. Eirik joined in the laughter, too, bowled over.

"The prettiest maiden of them all!" Eirik said, and Asgeir laughed even harder.

A flurry of laughter overcame him. He laughed to mock him, laughed as he knew his vengeance on Earp had come, and laughed since he found it of utmost amusement.

Just as he caught his breath to further insult his enemy more, he caught eyesight of someone else he thought he knew. A small, slender girl, who stared at him with the darkest eyes he had only seen from Sakka.

The girl stood there, a head shorter than him, black hair like silk thread, a pale face under a Pictish hood. She clasped her hands over her mouth, and Asgeir knew the blue veins that crisscrossed her hands as Sakka's.

Eirik, still taken by a fit of laughter, wiped a tear from his eye and put an arm around Asgeir. "Say, Asgeir – we should have a play, and Earp here be Thor, when he guised as a woman to retrieve Freya's necklace – no, maybe he can dress as Freya!"

Asgeir rushed past Eirik, and grabbed ahold of Sakka, lifted her up and held her against him.

"Sakka, it's really you! I knew I saw you there, before the thick of battle."

"Asgeir, I can't believe it, I heard you drowned," she said and held her head against his breast.

They stood there for a long while as it drizzled. Asgeir looked over his shoulder at Eirik.

"Keep who we need, set the others free. Put Earp in binds – we cannot trust him. Sell him straightaway and be done with it."

Asgeir brought Sakka to the byre, where he had been tied up and beaten by Earp so many months ago. *I should tie him up, and beat him now. But Sakka, by all the Gods, I am lucky.*

The lass stood there in the doorway, unsure. Her hair had grown matted and tangled. She had the unclean must of bog on her, and much grime crusted her fingers. She looked skinnier and her skin sallow.

"You kept my spirits up, Sakka. I knew if I defeated Haakon, I'd see you again."

She gave a weak smile as she crumpled down against the wall of the byre, arms crossed. "Thank you, Asgeir, but I just want to go home."

"You're free now, Sakka."

"What use is it, if I cannot go home?"

Sakka wrung her mouth at the sight of Asgeir. Haakon must have caught the Finnmen before they vanished into the hinterlands of the mountains.

"My father, Haakon hated him after his dance at the hall," Sakka said, but stared at Asgeir tearless.

"You needn't more," he said.

"He hated you," she said.

Asgeir had taken her maidenhood while her husband-to-be had been out hunting. With her marriage spoiled, her father had throttled him, and he had barely escaped alive.

"Your mother lives?"

"She's been sold to the slave market in Dubh Linn. I'll never see her again."

Asgeir shook his head. "I never thought I'd see you again, and now I have."

Sakka dry-sobbed. She leaned her back against the wall. "I've been eating nothing but bugs and frogs. I was so hungry, Asgeir. I thought of self-murder for weeks, but each time I stood at the edge of a cliff, the bear-father whispered in my ear to have hope. If I had known you were the one to defeat Haakon, and take his land, I would have left the hills sooner.

"I just want to see the walruses again," she said as she plucked a pair of bone needles from her side-pouch. She stuck them under her lip and roared. Asgeir laughed, and she did, too.

"Stay here with me," Asgeir said.

Sakka closed her eyes and leaned her head against his shoulder. She spat out her walrus tusks and kissed him as the rain pitter-pattered the byre-roof.

"By Frigga, I will never agree to you having another wife," Saga said.

They sat in Asgeir's hall in the early evening, as his newfound thralls prepared a feast. Saga bobbed her leg over her knee, her hair loose, her gracile hands ringless, her face cheerless. She knotted some silk thread within her fingers until it resembled a spider's web. Her madder-red dress, bare of brooches. She would not wear another until Asgeir had gifted her a new pair. He had hoped his mother would bring over his grandmother's pair for the wedding. And a gold ring to swear the oath of marriage on, to Frigga, Odin's wife.

Asgeir sat next to her, wrapped in a fringed cloak in the same manner as his father. He dressed as the Gaels, bare-legged, and wore a silk headband.

His father, clad as he, sat cross-armed and would let out a "ha!". Next to him, Godifu sat.

"In fact, I find it insulting that you suggested that – an affront to Frigga, and a blight on our future marriage."

Godifu, eyebrows raised and mouth parted, placed a hand on Saga's forearm. "The way of the Danes is not so difficult."

"I'm not a Dane, you Saxon, and I am not going their way."

"Surely, a follower of the Heathen Gods can agree to it," Godifu said.

"Not my 'Heathen' Gods, Saxon. I will not have my husband laying with his thralls."

"She isn't my thrall," Asgeir said.

"He's already sent her squealing!" Hallgeir said with a gusty laugh. "Could hear her cat-shrieks down by the pier even!"

Godifu slapped her husband's arm. "That's rude, Hallgeir – you're not helping this."

Saga flexed her fingers, the silk thread pressed into her flesh. "And I am to raise some she-thrall's bastards? By Frigga, I will not."

"The lad had some hard fights," Hallgeir said. "He needed the comfort. We all do."

"I will hear no more of it, for it is insulting. May I remind you, Hallgeir of Lothlend, that my father was Jarl of Seim, royalty of the Hordar people, back to the times when they war-wandered with the Goths, the Lombards, and before that, my forefathers served the Roman army, and brought back troves of gold. An affront to my blood, and my odalmen will wake from their graves. And what am I even supposed to do while they do … that? Sing loudly to myself so I cannot hear that she-thrall howl like a hound?"

"She won't budge on this – stubborn, but you want a stubborn wife," Hallgeir said. "You had your pleasure with the Finngirl. Let it alone."

"It's not for pleasure," Asgeir said. *Saga.* Her stern jaw, her sloped nose, her thin blond eyebrows. Her gray eyes iron-like in the firelight. He remembered her as she sang the healing rune for him, while he laid prone, spear wound in his chest, back at Borgund. He touched the scarring flesh under his tunic.

"So that we know my son has no duties to bastards or orphans, Haakon sired no children, correct?" Hallgeir asked.

"No," Saga said. "He suffered a wound in the land of the Wends before we married. Freya hadn't ever blessed us that way. I will not speak ill of the dead, but methinks that the Norns have spun fate differently for us. Hallgeir – and Asgeir – take this royal dowry and I will bear you highborn grandchildren. But I will spew the harshest snake-venom if my husband frolics about with some she-thrall."

The Norns spun Asgeir a tangled skein. In just one short week, Arild, Sakka's husband-to-be, lay dead at his feet. His lust had overcome him with Sakka, and their threads twined to a yarn. Now there, on Haakon's farm, with Haakon and Arild dead, Sakka and Saga wove into him. Auntie Bjorg would visit for the wedding, surely. She could unravel his fate. But none of this would have happened if Hallgeir had settled his debt to Ulf. And now, he would marry Saga to fulfill his father's wish.

Marriage is not for love. Father's right. I just wish Saga would let me with Sakka. But if I am to take my life into my own hands, I must have powerful friends. And Saga would be utmost a powerful friend.

Asgeir sucked in air as he spoke. "I agree, Saga."

She nodded, and stared at him.

I don't know if she believes me. And how am I going to tell Sakka?

"It is agreed then, by Frigga, my boy will be married! Come, my love," Hallgeir said to Godifu, "they should have some time alone."

Hallgeir and Godifu left.

Asgeir and Saga sat in silence for a long while. She scooted over to him, unbuttoned the collar of his tunic by the jet pearl button, and gawked at his spear wound. With a smooth, warm finger, she ran it over nine times as she whispered to herself.

"No fester. Just a scar. You will live."

"I thank you, Saga the Healer."

She sighed heavily and leaned a forehead on his shoulder and rested it there.

My deeds have granted me this woman. I acted with honor. You were right, father.

At the cairn upon the hilltop over Asgeir's farm, Sakka stood with a wreath of flowers, marigold and primrose. She laid them at the stones and went silent, head bowed. A silent prayer. The elves of the land, or what the Finns named them.

"I am so far from the graves of my forefathers," she said to Asgeir.

"As am I," he said, with a soapstone cup of the last sour wine. "Yet the elves of the land must know us now that we are here."

"They will know our children," Sakka said, and Asgeir blanched.

"I must tell you now, then," he said.

"Your father summoned you to the hall, what happened there?"

"I am to marry Saga the Healer."

Sakka went crestfallen.

"I asked if she would allow me a second wife, and she will not, as part of our deal."

"And you didn't even ask me about that first?" Sakka asked. "I am no thrall to you now."

"My father wished I marry a woman of high rank."

Sakka sank down against the standing-stone, her arms crossed, her eyes unfocused.

"Now I am free, but what of it?" she said with a near yell. "I have nowhere to go and be free to. Shall I swim back to Norway?"

"We can arrange you passage, though I do not want you to leave."

"And then where? How can I ever go home? Some viking will seize me and sell me again."

Asgeir knelt next to her. She intertwined his fingers with hers. He shivered at her frigid touch.

"Then live with us, as a helper."

"I suppose so, since I have naught else to go, but I will be no secret lover, if that is your hope," she said, rose, and walked off.

With a churn of his heart, he poured wine and dabbed it against the stones. "For the elves, and for Frigga, who guided me in marriage. I trust you."

The lamplight lit the hall in the late evening. The longfire had died after the feast, its cinders still flickering and coals still glowing. The thralls ferried in whale meat, butchered from a fresh carcass, while others busied outside to salt whatever could be salvaged before the sea-beast rotted on the beach.

Asgeir sat with Saga, still yet unwed, but locked in arms. His father and Godifu sat across from them. At the far end, Rudolf, his mistress with a babe-at-breast.

Rudolf stood up, holding a drinking-horn with an antler-carved rim. He raised it high.

"The God Freyr himself has ordained this – my first forebear – I, Rudolf High-Hat of Svearia, has earned, and now claim, the title of Jarl of Orkney and Hjaltland. All that refuse to accept my destiny will be kowtowed. We will drink now, to peace, before Harald will bring us war. But I will lead you, and under my leadership, the men of Orkney and Hjaltland will remain free."

The men in the hall cheered, thrust their drinks forward, and a chant of "Rudolf" sounded. Rudolf took a slight bow as the chant quieted, then sipped the horn and passed it to his nearest warrior, who stood up and sipped, and passed it down. As the horn traveled down the table, the soft note of a lyre fluttered in the hall. Ordenhait, the former bard, now Skald, from Barr Island entered the hall.

"For yet still many songs of me to sing about, and this skald, now mine, has a honeyed voice," he said.

Ordenhait strummed his lyre, the gut strings shivering over the amber bridge. He hummed himself in tune and then sang:

Many gulls and crows fed,
When Rudolf painted Orkney red.
Haakon's jarldom of sand,
Crumbled by High-hat's fierce hand.

The guests cheered as Rudolf clapped hard, and he beckoned Ordenhait up to the High-Seat.

"Sing one of my son," he said.

Ordenhait cleared his throat, sipped mead from a small soapstone cup, and sang:

Upon the borg's hill,

A ghastly blood spill.

Brave Arild felled countless men,

As Sigurd dived into fen.

Haakon the coward shifted blame,

For the deed of the hero's shame.

Ordenhait bowed, his hatless, bald head gleaming in the candlelight from the hanging-lamp. The guests cheered as Saga handed Asgeir the horn. He just stared at the mead and she placed a hand on his knee. Rudolf hadn't clapped.

"Tell me, skald, what do you mean that Haakon shifted the blame?"

"Why," Ordenhait said as he spotted Asgeir, his mouth parted. "He had someone else act as beheader."

"Who?" Rudolf asked, as the guests quieted.

Before Ordenhait could answer, Asgeir sprang up. The horn slammed into the table and splashed mead about the guests across from him.

"It was I, Rudolf," he shouted. "And I cannot live with this lie!"

Murmurs and whispers ruffled throughout the guests. Saga put a hand over her mouth, but shook her head, got up, and tugged Asgeir by the arm to leave. Rudolf jutted his jaw out.

"You are hereby outlawed to Iceland, Asgeir, son of Hallgeir, the Viking-Gael. You have nine days to leave Orkney. Sell your land. You are never to return."

Asgeir and Saga left, while Rudolf stood as still as the dragonhead of a prow save for the drinking-horn that trembled in his frozen hand.

"Just as well, Saga," Asgeir said as he left the hall, "we will be better off without these quarreling jarls. We will build a life together, unneedful of them."

"A new life for us, dear," she said. "I am in agreement – let us leave all this ugliness behind forever and live under Freyr and Freya. It's what the Norns spun for us."

Asgeir and Hallgeir stood astride the wharf where the knarr rocked in the choppy waves. The ship had been loaded with their belongings, beasts, and followers. He pointed to where the thralls could drop a heavy rug, and Asgeir, for an eyeblink, thought of Fina. *She really did hide herself well. I'll miss that lass.*

Hallgeir, Godifu at his side, placed a hand on Asgeir's shoulder.

"I hear Iceland has green land. There's much space, and horses thrive," Godifu said.

"I don't intend to stay long."

Hallgeir stroked his beard.

"I'll not be an outlaw forever. I'll return home someday, whether it's the South Isles or Norway."

"Understood," Hallgeir said with a grin. "For our part, we will return to the South Islands. I see the way the wind blows – I don't trust Rudolf. But I know Harald will send a fleet, and I must warn the King of Lothlend, for the South Isles will not be spared from Harald either."

"I will amass men," Asgeir said. "And we will keep our islands free."

A tear rolled down Hallgeir's cheek.

"Go, son, to Iceland. Get married. And make many friends. When you are ready, I will be waiting for you in the South Isles, with ships, weapons, men."

"I understand, father. We will never be puppies."

"But sea-wolves – side by side, in our pack. They walk with the trickster, but we will walk with Odin, as the Ulfhednir, the wolf warriors of yore, and Harald will regret defying Hallgeir, housecarl to Lothlend, and Asgeir of Eigg, the Viking Gael. Farewell, my son."

"And father – please, if you ever meet Rolf Ulfsson, show him mercy, for as it was Haakon that killed Arild, it was Ulf that killed Odd."

Hallgeir bit his lip and gave a slight nod. "I suppose for you, my son, I can stay my sword."

Asgeir boarded the ship and placed a hand on the rudder. Eirik and Hallgeir pushed her out to tide, Eirik hopped onboard next to Sakka. Hallgeir leaned over the gunwhale to scratch Svartganger under his chin, and with a wave from the Gael-Slayer, the shoreline of Rousay vanished among the hazy sea.

CHAPTER X

The Afterwalker

For many vika, they traveled against the western current. Gray sky, gray waves, gray eyes of Saga as she huddled herself against him in the coldness of the open sea. They sailed by way north, far from Cape Wrath, until the boggy island of Ljodhus came to view. They havened in the harbor there, and after a night of rest, they journeyed forth to Iceland.

A wooded bay graced the horizon, with wisps of smoke painting the trees white. They landed on shore, where a simple turf-built house sat. Saga approached with Asgeir, her scales in hand, and there they vied lead weights against the silver that Rudolf paid them for Toke's farm. After they found their home, far inland and upstream, they dwelled in tents until the Gaelic slaves built their turf-walled house over the days. When the walls seemed sturdy enough, they flipped the hull of the ship upon it as a roof. As the slaves fastened the roof, Eirik nudged Asgeir.

"The harbormaster sold us an old man," he said.

Asgeir found a lanky, tall, gray-haired man stacking turf blocks. His downcast eyes never met his.

"Many winters he may be, he's still working as hard as any other," Asgeir said.

"I just thought it odd to see such an old thrall."

The chasms on his old leathery cheeks. The wispy gray hair. The hardened thews and rippling veins that belied his age. The mariner's hands.

Asgeir thought back to his earlier visions, of the afterwalker that hobbled across the seabed toward him. The drowned man. The dweller of Ran's realm.

Ulf the Old stood there before him. Asgeir knew him. He was as sure as Thor's hammer struck giants dead.

You've heeded my need for a true Viking to show me what my father wouldn't.

"You're the afterwalker, Ulf."

With a creak of his hunched back, Ulf the Old, sea-legged, staggered toward him.

"Bygones, you ancient sea-dog," Asgeir said. "I need the help of an unchained wolf. You're a thrall no longer. You're free. And we're going to return to Hjaltland and Orkney and Norway with a fleet of vikings. There's no honor among men these days – and we ought to teach them what it means."

A slight smile formed from Ulf's thin lips.

I will rebuild the Sea-Bitch's crew, and we will ravage the shores of Harald's realm, for I am the Viking Gael, and we'll pillage Rudolf and Harald alike.

TO BE CONTINUED

The Viking Gael will return in book 3: The Sea King, in 2024! *Please Review this Book!*

If you enjoyed The Viking Gael Saga then please leave me a review. A simple "I liked it!" is sufficient. This helps bring positive attention to the book and my work, so I really appreciate it!

SUBSCRIBE TO MY NEWSLETTER

SCAN THE QR CODE BELOW

THE SEA KING

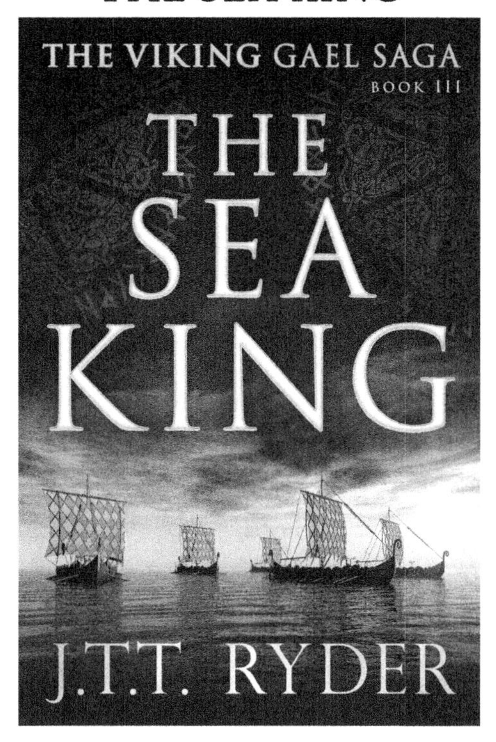

Outlawed but undeterred, Asgeir will return as the Sea King.

After his banishment to Iceland, Asgeir forges alliances to vie against his enemies.

With the aid of his old captain, he commands a crew of vikings, and reins as the Sea King. In the bloody waters of Scotland and Ireland, he will earn the respect of friend and foe alike as the fearsome Viking Gael.

COMING 2024

Pre-Order Now

HAG OF THE HILLS

"Nothing is unconquerable; even our gods can die."

When the Hillmen murder his entire clan, Brennus is left no other choice but to live up to his family's legacy and seek retribution.

Now, he must survive endless hordes of invaders and magic-wielding sidhe, aided by a band of shifty mercenaries and an ancient bronze sword.Will he succeed?

Find out for yourself in "Hag of the Hills", the first instalment in the completed "Bronze Sword Cycles" historical fiction duology set in 200 B.C., steeped in Celtic mythology and culture.

Available now on all major retailers

THE LION OF SKYE

There can only be one Lion of Skye!

Vidav must defeat his brother in order to fulfil his oath to kill the Queen of the Hillmen.

If he does not fulfil his oath, his clan will be unavenged, and the Isle of Skye will remain under enemy rule.

If he does fulfil his oath, his brother may die.

Even worse, a dragon has been flying over Skye...

The Lion of Skye is the epic conclusion to the Bronze Sword Cycles duology, a historical fiction adventure set in 200 B.C. on the Isle of Skye, steeped in Celtic mythology and culture.

Available now on all major retailers

TOMB OF THE BLUE DEMONS

The Druid Ambicatos embarks on a journey of intrigue that quickly turns into war, when he arrives in war-torn Italia, under siege by the Carthaginians.

While the war rages, Ambicatos falls for a mysterious woman some call the Sorceress, who claims she has discovered the sight, the power of the Underworld.

Ambicatos must fight friend and foe alike in this epic novella, a prequel to Hag of the Hills, the Bronze Sword Cycles duology.

This novella is part of Celtic historical fiction series The Bronze Sword Cycles, set in 200 BC.

Available now on all major retailers

ABOUT THE AUTHOR

Joseph Thomas Thor Ryder is an archaeologist and author of the historical fiction. He is a published author of Viking archaeology, and a doctoral candidate specializing in the Viking Age and Celtic Iron Age. He resides in Norway where he conducts archaeological research and writes historical fiction.

APPENDIX

Afterword

I am an archaeologist of the Viking Age. That means that I study the past through material culture – what people physically left behind. This can be anything from a sword in a burial, to a series of house foundations, to a handful of coins, to some charred grain to radiocarbon date. The Viking Age is my area of expertise, but I am by no means incapable of faults. I attempted to be as historically accurate as possible. Unfortunately, the deeper you dig into the past, the deeper you realize that total historical accuracy is impossible. Napoleon Bonaparte (paraphrase) said that history is a series of fables agreed upon. It is actually a series of interpretations debated. Therefore, this story is my interpretation of how life may have been like in the Viking Age, around the mid-late 9th century AD. It is not the only interpretation, or even my only interpretation.

Dating and historiography

This story takes place in AD 870. This is right at the eve of the (traditional, not necessarily historical) unification of Norway, attested to in many later sources such as the Sagas. Regardless of the historicity of Harald Finehair, Norway was still likely divided up by a series of petty kingdoms and/or jarldoms. People from western Norway were likely colonizing the islands of Scotland, such as the Orkneys, Shetland, and the Hebrides, though archaeological evidence is much stronger for Viking presence in the subsequent 10th century. Nevertheless, Viking incursions likely led to the unification of the Picts and Scots and the cultural disappearance of the former. The Faroes would have been colonized, and Iceland was discovered but (probably) not yet colonized. Dublin and other areas of Ireland were under control by the Norse, where proto-urban trade towns flourished, and Norse, along with Hiberno-Norse peoples, would have a presence around the island for the next several hundred years until the Norman conquest. To the south, the Danes were very much busy in England, but this series will not concern the Danelaw or Jorvik. At least, not yet.

South Isles, the – The Hebrides

Historical figures

Harald Finehair (850 – 932) – traditionally known as the first King of Norway, who unified the petty kingdoms and jarldoms of Norway as well as Norse-colonized islands of Scotland. His historicity is disputed; but I like to think he existed.

King of Lothlend, the – Lothlend, or Laithlinn, is a kingdom mentioned in the Irish Annals, contemporary with our period. Likely, it designated some political union of Vikings from Norway. Just where this kingdom was located has been disputed by scholars for decades. For this series, I located it in the South Isles (Hebrides), where I personally believe it was located.

Printed in Great Britain
by Amazon